ALPHA PROTECTOR WOLF

BRIDGE HOLLOW SHIFTERS 3

SAMANTHA LEAL

CONTENTS

Chapter 1   1
Chapter 2   7
Chapter 3   12
Chapter 4   20
Chapter 5   28
Chapter 6   35
Chapter 7   41
Chapter 8   45
Chapter 9   51
Chapter 10   59
Chapter 11   65
Chapter 12   72
Chapter 13   81
Chapter 14   90
Chapter 15   99
Chapter 16   104
Chapter 17   113
Chapter 18   121

CHAPTER 1

The summer months were beginning to end, and the chill in the air of Bridge Hollow was rolling in faster than any of the residents had ever known.

Dash stood on the edge of Main Street, smoking a cigarette and watching the world flash by. His dark eyes scanned the crowds from under his hooded brow. The tourists were still lingering, and the skiers were still making their way up the mountain, but he now saw a different turn in the energy of the town.

This place was getting darker and more menacing by the minute.

So much had happened since the beginning of the year. It was hard to believe that fall was already here. Especially considering all the strange happenings that had plagued them for months on end.

He took a drag on his smoke, exhaled, and then dropped it onto the ground before he crunched it out with the tip of his boot. He ran a hand through his jet-black hair and a small growl escaped his lip. He didn't know if he was tired or frustrated. He had been wanting to go home early and not get sucked into another late night, but as the sun was beginning to fall, it felt as if there were so many empty hours stretching out ahead of him that home was the last place he wanted to be.

He took one last look up and down Main Street. The streetlamps were coming on slowly, and he could smell the freshly lit fires from the bars and restaurants wafting around town. The bars and taverns were starting to sound lively, and he craved a beer and a whiskey more than he had in weeks.

He reached up and rubbed his hand across his jaw. Even though the injuries were long healed, he could still feel the ache deep within his bones. He had been the unlucky one of his wolf pack when it had come to a recent fight with a rival gang of shifter bears, but luckily for him, they had buried the hatchet. They had bigger things to worry about in Bridge Hollow than wolves and bears at each other's throats. Now that the weather was changing, plants and trees were diseased and mass populations of animals were dying, it was clear to them all that they had a greater threat on the horizon.

Dash clicked his jaw and the ache began to subside. He had nothing to fear from the bears any longer, and he and his kind were more than welcome in their businesses and homes.

He turned and began to walk down Main Street toward a familiar warm glow coming from inside a wooden building. He could hear the music and smell the smoke and booze from a block away, and it made him smile. For all the trouble that seemed to happen here, he sure as hell loved his town, and he was determined to do whatever he could to save it.

He reached the entrance of the bar and looked up to the sign above the doorway.

. . .

SHIFTER'S BLISS

IT WAS ONE OF THE MOST POPULAR SPOTS IN TOWN, BUT IF THE tourists and many of the residents truly knew what went down there, he wasn't sure if it would make them want to go more or drive them away for good.

He pushed open the door and stepped inside. It was a typical Bridge Hollow night, and many familiar faces were already inside after a hard day at work. He nodded to a few of the bear clan that were gathered around a corner booth, and he smiled as he approached the bar and saw the owner, Ryder, waiting on customers.

"Evening, Dash," Ryder said with a friendly smile as Dash pulled out a high bar stool and sat down.

"Evening," Dash returned.

He eased himself out of his heavy leather jacket and slung it across the backrest, before he leaned onto the wooden bar top with his thick, muscular arms and reached into his pocket for another smoke.

"What can I get you?" Ryder asked as he stopped in front of him and began to clear away the empty glasses on the countertop.

"I'll take a beer," Dash said as he clamped the cigarette between his teeth and lifted the lighter up to let the flame catch the end.

Ryder had been one of the bears he had fought with only weeks before. But now that they had eased tension between their packs, they had become fast friends.

He set the beer down on the bar in front of Dash, and Dash smiled and thanked him. He picked up the bottle and took a long, satisfying swig, before he exhaled and turned around to survey the rest of the bar. It was a bit quieter than normal, even with all the familiar faces, and Dash was sure some of his own pack would arrive soon to sink a few after work beers. He took another drag of his smoke and tapped his foot against the bar to the beat of the rock music blaring out of the jukebox as he looked toward the other side of the room.

It seemed darker over to the right, as if some of the lights weren't working the way they should have been. The booths that lined the edges of the room all had at least one bulb above them and some along the walls, but there was one in the far corner that was completely dark, as if all the lights around it hadn't been turned on.

He squinted as he kept looking and he felt a dip in his stomach as he realized a man was there, slumped over the table in the center of the booth and completely out for the count.

"Oh Christ," Dash laughed as he took another swig of his beer. "What the hell happened to him?"

Ryder followed his line of sight and stilled for a moment. The pair of them looked over to the sleeping man, at how drunk and buckled he looked, and Ryder smiled and shook his head before they both suddenly sensed at the same time that something wasn't right.

Dash looked at Ryder, and then he sniffed the air.

The wolf inside of him growled and he felt the rush of energy and adrenaline that came with fear and excitement. The wolf wanted to spring free and come out to play, but not for a carefree reason. He wanted to come out to protect.

Dash quickly got to his feet and subdued the growls escaping from his lips. At the same time, Ryder's eyes flashed with something gold, and the sound of chairs scraping back against the wooden floor echoed around the room. The rest of the bears had sensed it too, and they were stomping across the floor toward Ryder and Dash at the bar.

The group of shifters, all bears and one wolf, stood and

looked at the drunk in the corner. He easily could have been asleep. He was hunched over the table, his arms hanging limp and loose down by his side. His face was turned toward the wall and his drink was still sitting next to him as if he just hadn't been able to finish it. But with their heightened senses, once they had all locked in on him, the shifters of Bridge Hollow knew this man wasn't asleep at all.

Because they could smell death.

Dash felt the prickle of dread creep up the back of his neck and the wolf inside of him worked its way forward again. His eyes flashed green and he felt the animal wanting to emerge. It was on high alert and ready for battle. He let his wolf come to the surface and his glinting green eyes stared back at Ryder and the other bears. They all looked as concerned as he was, and with each step he took forward, the stench got stronger.

He stopped in front of the booth and could see the shards of broken glass on the floor under the table. His eyes looked up to the light fixture above it and he could see that the bulb had completely burst. The one on the wall had too. SO, it wasn't just simply the case that Ryder had forgot to turn them on.

His blood started to burn red hot and he was on high alert. A growl escaped his lips as he sniffed the air and then looked back down to the dead man sprawled across the table.

He reached out and felt the side of his neck, checking for a pulse. But as he already knew, there wasn't anything he could find. His skin was already cold. Unnaturally so. And he knew then that this was not just a freak accident. The man hadn't died of natural causes. Something terrible had happened. And what was worse… no one in the room had noticed.

Ryder came to stand by Dash's side, and they exchanged a glance before Dash moved the man's head slightly to expose the other side of his neck. When they both saw what was there, Dash instinctively growled and bared his teeth, even though he was still in his human form.

Ryder's bear was clearly fighting inside of him too, and they both growled and howled, as their eyes came alive with the animals within them.

On the other side of the dead man's neck were two perfect puncture wounds, lightly dripping blood.

Someone had done this to him.

He had been murdered.

"What could have done this?" Dash whispered as he ran a shaking hand down his face.

Ryder didn't reply, but that didn't change anything. They all knew what was going on...

The threat that had been coming to Bridge Hollow was getting stronger... and by the looks of it, something darker was now finally here.

CHAPTER 2

Jannie bumped along the uneven mountain road, swerving her truck from left to right as she tried to steady the map against the steering wheel. She had been lost on these roads for what felt like forever now, having had left town without asking for help.

She sighed and pulled over to the side of the road, under a patch of pine trees, and gritted her teeth as she rested the map on the wheel properly and gripped it with both her hands.

The lines all seemed to blur into one. Red, blue, green… who the hell knew what she was looking at, but she knew she couldn't be far. The app she had booked the cabin with had the directions stored, but she didn't have any signal to access it, and she was growing more and more irritated by the second. She furrowed her brow and looked closer, managing to figure out which road she was on, and that she was heading East.

"Right," she sighed again as she threw the map onto the seat beside her and rolled out her shoulders. "It should just be up here on the left…" She sounded apprehensive as she said it, but she didn't have any choice but to keep going and trying to find her new home for the next six weeks.

She slammed the truck into drive, checked her mirrors and pulled back out onto the winding country roads. She kept her eye on her driving, but also couldn't help but gasp as she took in the views all around her. The mountain, and the range around it, were absolutely stunning; she had never seen anything so enchanting in her entire life. The size of the trees that rose out of the ground were awe inspiring, and they darkened the roads as she drove by. The lakes that popped out of the green landscape were all crystal blue, and the mountains that skimmed the clouds were snowcapped and fantastical in their own way.

When she finally began to approach a turn off, she breathed a sigh of relief and sat forward as she gripped the wheel and began to turn. The road dipped and began to wind down a slope, and she navigated the truck slowly to ensure she didn't find herself going off road and landing in a ditch. As the road got lower and lower, the trees began to open out and she smiled as she saw the amazing vista spreading out ahead of her.

This was what she had come for.

This was the cabin she had found and fallen in love with.

"Yes," she grinned to herself as she pulled up outside and turned off the engine.

She opened the driver's door and stepped out into the crisp mountain air. The hairs on the back of her neck tingled as she spun around on the spot and took it all in.

The cabin had been on a rental app, and she had been overjoyed when she had found it. She had been studying and wanting to come to Bridge Hollow for so long, and once she saw that they had started leasing private properties on both long and short-term lets, she had finally plucked up the courage to get herself out there for real.

Jannie had been longing for an adventure for so long, and after a recent break up with yet another bullish guy, she now had her chance to take time for herself and find her true inspiration.

She looked up at the cabin. It was everything she had hoped for. Small and charming, rustic and authentic. But it was also newly renovated and looked like a little dream spot from the pictures she had found online. It was only one bedroom, separate bathroom, and also an adjoining shower room to the bedroom, but it also had a larger, open-plan kitchen and living space with a vaulted mezzanine floor above the living area which looked out over the lake and the mountains beyond. On the pictures, it had been filled with big, bouncy floor cushions and a bookshelf with lots of old books, and so, Jannie had already decided that was where she was going to set up her workstation and spend her days writing.

She smiled as she took it all in. The cabin was secluded and idyllic, the lake behind it was as blue and clear as the sky, and she could see other little homes dotted around it in the distance. This was a beautiful part of the world, and she felt truly blessed that she was finally here.

She grabbed her bags out of the trunk, slung them over her shoulder and headed toward the front door.

When she turned the key and stepped inside, she certainly wasn't disappointed. She saw the wonderful little cabin which she had adored in the photographs, and she was so pleased the owner had stayed true and not tried to pass it off as something better than it was.

She let her bags fall to the floor as she walked through the hallway to the back of the house. where the kitchen and living area opened out and the huge windows and doors along the back of the building let in light and stunning views of the lake.

"Perfect," she grinned with delight as she clasped her hands together.

She turned and looked at the kitchen counter and could see a welcome note and a bottle of wine. She smiled as she walked over, picked up the note and began to read…

Welcome to your little slice of Bridge Hollow heaven!
We hope you'll be very happy here. Please enjoy this
wine on us. If you need anything, don't hesitate to give us a
shout!

"That's so cute," she smiled to herself as she set the note back down on the counter and reached for the wine. It was a dark bottle and must have been a red, and she noticed that the label had a picture of a bear and wolf chasing each other.

"How apt," she laughed with an eye roll. She was more than familiar with the legends of this town, and it was precisely the reason she had been so eager to come.

She headed back out to the car and pulled out a cardboard box in which she had stored her groceries. She hitched it high on her hip, and locked the truck, and when she went back into the cabin, she closed and locked the front door.

"Welcome home, Jannie," she smiled. "To this next little chapter."

She walked back through to the kitchen and set the box down, and then she faltered for a moment before she suddenly felt the overwhelming feeling of being alone.

She swallowed and made sure that she wouldn't cry.

She had come on this adventure alone on purpose, and she wasn't about to chicken out now.

She glanced over at the wine and swiped the bottle

toward her before she opened the drawers and cupboards to find a corkscrew and glass. As she poured one for herself, she made herself a promise that this would be the only time she doubted her decision; from now on, she was going to be the strong, independent woman she knew she could be.

She didn't need Dylan. He had been bad for her from the start; he had been a bully and a liar. She had done the right thing by leaving him and their toxic relationship behind. She didn't need a man to depend on; she wanted to look after herself. Dylan had always made her feel as if she wasn't good enough, and he regularly tried to destroy her confidence. But not now. She had dumped his ass, regrouped, found her fire and decided to take this trip to re-spark her imagination and explore something that had long intrigued her.

Now that she was here, there was no way she was backing out.

She took a sip of the wine and smiled. It was warm and instantly settled her nerves. She cradled the glass in her palm and with her free hand, she scooped up one of her bags and walked toward her new bedroom. It was time for her to unpack and make herself at home.

CHAPTER 3

Once she had put her clothes in the closet, unpacked the food into the cupboards and the refrigerator, and had rested with another glass of wine for ten minutes, Jannie decided it was finally time to explore the mezzanine.

She had been saving the best for last, and she couldn't wait to get up there and immerse herself in setting up her office. For the next six weeks, she had the cabin on lease, and she was hopeful that, within that time, she would be able to explore the town of Bridge Hollow, meet some interesting people, and get a good foundation for the book she had wanted to write for as long as she could remember.

Jannie loved the idea of shifters. She had read and studied the myth for years and was truly a believer. She knew many people didn't have much faith when it came to the paranormal, or of anything outside of what they had been conditioned to believe, but Jannie had always been drawn to things that others couldn't explain.

When she was younger, she had heard so many tales about this mountain town. She remembered her grandmother telling her stories late at night when she went to spend the weekends with her, and of how her grandfather had been here once long, long ago. It had sparked something inside of her that she had never been able to shake, and now that she was finally here, it was as if she were ticking off a huge section of her bucket list.

She wanted to write a book, and she wanted to know if the legends of the shifters were real. It had almost been like a sign from God when she had been watching the news one day, not long after her breakup from Dylan, and had heard the town mentioned. She had sat forward and turned up the volume, listening intently to what the presenter was saying.

She heard the words *die offs, strange weather phenomena, mystery* and *disappearance*. And as soon as she pulled out her laptop and began to search the town, she was sucked back in all over again and she found that her obsession hadn't faded.

It had all come together when she had been given the opportunity to take a sabbatical from work, and she had been saving long enough to afford a good vacation. Lucky for her, instead of traveling to Europe like she had always planned, she decided to lease the cabin on an amazing deal, head out East and see what she could find in the mountains. It was a productive move. She was spending less, and she was going to hopefully find her inspiration and finally write the novel she always thought she had in her.

It was a win, win.

She climbed the step ladder up to the mezzanine floor and smiled when she saw how perfect it matched the photographs on the listing. It was a large space, but with not a whole lot of room to stand with the vault of the ceiling. It was clear that the owner had converted the attic into this awesome answer to extra space, and the windows and skylights all looked out over the lake, which flooded the room with light and made it feel big and open.

She wandered to the bookshelves and traced her fingertips along the spines of some of the old books. There were classics, more obscure titles and reference books, and a few newer looking, battered paperbacks that could have easily been left behind by other people who had rented the cabin over the years.

She looked at the comfy floor cushions scattered around the place, and then she saw the perfect space for a desk. She clapped her hands together and pulled the tape measure she had placed in her back pocket out, before she started to size up the area.

Outside, she heard the sounds of an engine and water spray, as if someone were jet skiing or power boating on the lake, and she found herself leaving her current task behind, dropping the tape measure to the floor, and stepping to the windows. She looked down to the lake and, as she had expected, she saw a man on a jet ski, bobbing up and down, and creating waves as he went.

"What are you up to...?" She smiled to herself as she watched him for a moment more. The lake wasn't overly large, but there were at least four other houses around it, dotted in equal distances. They all had their own docks, for a boat or a jet ski, and she noticed that only one of them was empty. It was the house directly opposite hers. She squinted to try and make out how many windows it had and if they were dark or lit up, but it was just a little too far to tell in the bright light of day.

She looked back to the man bobbing up and down on the water, and watched as he circled around, clearly enjoying himself and burning off some steam.

She smiled and then turned back to look at the tape measure lying on the floor before she had the bright spark of an idea.

If she wanted to get to know people in town, there was no time like the present.

. . .

She opened the back doors leading out onto the deck that ran along the back of the house and wandered onto the grass that led down to the jetty and the lake. The man was still hurtling around on the jet ski, circling the lake and making great white waves as he went. She stopped and held her hand up to shield her eyes from the sun, and in the sobering clean air, she wondered if it was the two glasses of wine that had made her so brave and eager to make friends.

She became aware that he had seen her, and she raised her hand in a shy wave. The jet ski circled once more and then the man waved back. Even from that distance, she could tell he had big muscles; his arms looked thick and tattooed, even from her viewing space on the dock, and it instantly made her prickle with tension.

Oh great, she thought. *Another bad boy... And here I thought I would be out here with simple mountain folk...*

She stood her ground and watched as he began to power the ski toward her, and he slowed down as he got closer and kicked up a spray as he brought it to a stop.

"Hey," he called to her. He was close to her dock, and she walked down to him slowly, still shielding her eyes from the sun and unable to see his face from powerful rays. The sun was behind him, and it was keeping his features hidden in his own shadow, but as she approached him, she slowly began to make him out, and her nerves began to jangle.

Man, oh man... This guy was HOT.

He smiled at her and leaned forward onto the handlebars of the jet ski. He was tall, dark and incredibly handsome, and the tattoos that snaked their way down his big, tanned forearms only made her heart flutter even more. He cocked his head to the side, and she closed her mouth, unsure of whether it had been fully hanging open in shock, or just slightly ajar.

"Hi," she managed to croak.

He was like nothing she had ever seen before. And it was worrying. He smiled again, and she was sure she saw a hint of green flash over his eyes.

"You okay?" he asked her with a wry smile.

She nodded and looked away, trying to gain her composure and not look like a complete fool. Her heart was pounding, and her palms were sweating. She had never had a reaction like this to anyone and she couldn't make sense of why it was happening to her here like this.

"I'm Jannie," she smiled finally as she prepared herself to look back at him. "I've just arrived and was looking for a bit of advice."

"I'm Dash," he said as he smiled up at her from the water. He seemed to be as confused as she was, but she couldn't tell if it was because he was interested in her, or because he thought she was an idiot. His eyes seemed to be boring into her, as if she were standing there naked and exposed for him to see. He was still bobbing up and down slowly on the jet ski and she could see that his legs were also tanned, wet and muscular.

"Hi," she smiled again shyly.

He raised his eyebrows and glared at her. It was clear, neither of them knew what to say, and were both as dumbfounded as the other.

"You here on vacation?" he finally asked her, to break the awkward silence.

Jannie nodded.

"Well, kind of," she blurted out at the same time. "I'm here for a while, to write a book."

His eyebrows raised again, and he looked down his nose at her.

"Oh really?" he asked cockily. "What are you, a journalist?"

Jannie wondered what she had done wrong, and she stepped back a little.

"No...," she stammered. "I mean, I have been in the past, but I'm not here on a story. I just wanted somewhere to hole up for a while and concentrate."

"And what better place to come than a town full of scandal?" he smirked. He was beginning to sound more and more standoffish by the second, but there was still something open about him.

Jannie crossed her arms over her chest and felt her walls springing up.

"Anyway," she said, to change the subject. "I don't know the area and was just wondering if you could point me in the right direction... I'm looking for somewhere I can buy a cheap desk. Nothing too fancy, just something that will see me over temporarily whilst I'm here."

"A desk?" he asked, almost condescendingly.

"Yeah," she said back sternly. "I need a desk to work, and there isn't one inside."

"What's wrong with the dining table?" he asked with a shrug.

She looked at him and found herself taking a step further back. This guy was intense. But he was also making her feel intense too. She felt like they could start arguing at any moment, as if fireworks were about to explode between them.

"I need a designated office space," she said matter-of-factly.

He shrugged his shoulders, as if he wasn't even interested, and then he looked out across the water and to the house on the other side of the lake. She could see, now that she was down there, that the windows all looked dark but the back door that opened out onto a veranda appeared to be open and a large black dog was lounging on the decking, looking out over the lake and watching his master.

"There are a few stores in town, antique shops and what have you," he said. "But I'm not sure what you'd find there. You may have to travel further afield. This isn't exactly the kind of town known for its furniture," he half laughed.

"Oh, okay," she said as she kicked at the dirt with the tip of her boot. "No worries, thanks for the information anyway."

She went to turn away, afraid he didn't want to speak with her any longer.

"But," he interjected. "I actually have one you could borrow… it's just sitting in my attic. It hasn't been used for years."

She looked up at him, at the green tinge of his eyes and the strong dark brows that were heavy on his head. Everything about him screamed danger, from the bulging muscles down to the tattoos. The black hair, the attitude she couldn't figure out, and the way his lip curled when he spoke to her as if he were playing a game, but there was something about him that intrigued her and made her want to know more.

"Really?" she asked nervously.

"Sure," he grinned. "Plus, it won't cost you a dime."

Jannie smiled and her shoulders relaxed. Since she had locked eyes with him, her guard had been up, and he had been a little rude to her too, but now, she was starting to feel as if she could let herself go.

The wine was still warm and buzzy inside of her, she looked back across the water to the house opposite and when she squinted, she could just about see that the dog was now standing, watching them, and she imagined his tail wagging.

"Is that your place?" she asked as she pointed across.

Dash looked back at her and nodded his head.

"So, it's not far, it's not a hassle for me to bring it across for you."

She bit her bottom lip and smiled sheepishly. He was so sexy, and now he was being hot and cold too, it was making her even more interested in who the hell this Dash was.

"Okay," she said. "As long as you don't mind, that would be great."

He nodded his head and revved the jet ski back to life.

"Give me a couple hours," he said as he began to move slowly across the water. "I'll come over at dusk."

He powered the machine to life and kicked up a spray of water as he blasted back out across the lake. Jannie stood fixed to the ground, completely dumbfounded and unsure of what the hell had just happened. It certainly wasn't what she had been expecting, but she was grateful, nonetheless.

Dash.

The helpful face of Bridge Hollow she hadn't known she needed.

She turned and headed back to the house before he had the chance to dock on his side and see her still staring. She smiled to herself as she stepped inside and closed the doors behind her without casting her eyes up to where he may be on the other side of the lake.

She had a couple hours, and then he would be bringing her a desk. She better make sure that the place was tidy, and she that was ready.

CHAPTER 4

She looked in the mirror and leaned in toward her reflection, checking her make-up and softly running her fingers through her hair. Jannie had never been the type of girl to get dolled up, but something about Dash was making her so nervous, she felt the intense need to make sure she at least spritzed on a bit of perfume before he arrived with the desk.

She left her new bedroom and wandered down the hallway to the living and kitchen area. The sun was starting to set, and it was glowing pink and gold across the lake. The view out from the windows and large glass doors was amazing, and she wrapped her arms around herself as she watched the beautiful colors reflecting on the water. The other two houses around the lake had lights on now, making it clear that they were occupied. Jannie waited for a moment and then looked toward Dash's cabin directly opposite. The large black dog was still lounging on the veranda, and it made her smile. The whole lake area was so incredibly peaceful, it was a lovely place to spend a lazy evening.

She looked toward the small wood burning stove with a

flume that went up and through the wall to the outside of the house. It was quite Scandinavian in style; she had never seen one in a home before. There were logs beside it in a wicker basket and she wondered how she could possibly light it without burning the place to the ground.

She turned a small lamp, beside the couch, on and turned on the television, creating some noise so the whole cabin wasn't silent. She had been so awkward around him when they had met on the lake, she hated the idea of him walking into her new home and the silence being deafening between them.

She found herself watching the lake again and looking for some kind of sign. But there wasn't any sort of movement or stirring, either on the water or in the trees beside Dash's cabin.

She bit her bottom lip and breathed in and out deeply. She had never been a fan of waiting for someone. Even though it wasn't a date, it reminded her of the same apprehension she experienced when she was on her way to meet a guy. She had been terrified when she had started dating Dylan, and the nerves before her first date with him had almost driven her mad. She remembered the sensation of her heart pounding fast and hard, the way her mouth went dry, and the fact that everything seemed to be happening around her in slow motion. She hadn't even heard a word he had said when they were speaking to each other across the table in the restaurant, and he had never let her forget it. He had always taunted her, always let her know that she was below him. He was dangerous in his own way, as well as a shitty person. He had been in trouble with the law and he had stolen and hurt people. But she had been sucked right in, and when she realized it was all wrong... somehow, it was too late. He wasn't going to let her out of it that easily.

Dylan had been bad.

He had been dangerous.

He had hurt her in so many ways, she knew she never wanted to be vulnerable to a man ever again. And she was determined to stick to her word.

She looked out across the lake again, and just as her eyes found the veranda and she saw that the dog was gone, a loud pounding knock pummeled her front door and she gasped.

"Shit!" She jumped as she clutched her chest.

She must have been daydreaming and remembering her bad dating past for much longer than she had realized. At least long enough for Dash to leave his cabin and make it all the way around the lake without her seeing him.

She laughed and looked behind her to the doorway and, sure enough, she could see the shape of his head through the frosted glass on the small window at the top of the front door.

She made her way to it and found herself running her hands through her hair again and adjusting her top. When she reached the door, she opened it wide, he was looking down at the ground but in an instant and he tilted his gaze up to hers, their eyes met again, and she felt a warm wave roll over her entire body.

"Hey," he said with a wry smile.

He looked good. Better than he had at the lake. He was wearing low slung jeans, a tight black t-shirt, and a leather jacket over his broad shoulders. His hair had been washed and he smelled strongly of a delicious cologne. He looked clean and fresh, tanned and comfortable in his own skin. And either, he was on his way out after he had been to see her or he had really made an effort to impress. She found herself smiling shyly again as she stepped to the side so he could come in.

She noticed the dog was beside him, sitting upright, being

good as gold. His eyes were an intense blue and his coat was a luxurious black.

"Hello," She smiled as she bent forward to reach out and give him a rub on the head, "and who is this?"

"This is Jet." Dash smiled as he reached out and started to roughhouse with the dog. He looked like a wolf, a playful, magnificently handsome, beast, and he was clearly very close to his owner.

"He's gorgeous," Jannie said as she stood back up and began to walk down the hallway toward the kitchen. "He's more than welcome to come in."

Dash whistled and the dog began to trot down the hallway too. Jannie wandered into the living area and turned around to face Dash. When she saw him walking into the room with her, her heart began to pound again.

He looked so good.

But he was clearly a bad guy. And she was done with bad guys.

No more bad! No Jannie! No!

"Wow," he exhaled as he looked at the vaulted ceiling high above them. "This is much nicer than I thought it would be."

Jannie didn't know if that was a positive or an insult.

"Oh yeah?" she asked as she made her way to the refrigerator.

She pulled out a beer and waved it in front of him and he put his hands on his hips.

"For your trouble?" she said.

"Sure, why not," smiling as he reached out and took it from her. "Thanks."

She was about to go looking for the bottle opener, but Dash quickly and confidently used the edge of the island in the kitchen to pop the cap free and then he let it scatter across the countertop. Jannie reached for her glass of wine. She had poured herself another red and was just below half of the bottle, but she felt alert and on her guard. She was just glad that the edge of her nerves had been taken away and she was able to chat with ease with this hunk of a man.

"Thanks so much for your help," she said as she looked around and realized that the desk was nowhere in sight.

"Well… about that…," Dash said as he clamped his teeth together and looked a little apologetic.

Jannie smiled and put her hand on her hip.

"I kind of fucked up," he said. "I was getting it down from the attic and managed to knock one of the legs off the damn thing. I need a day or two to fix it and it'll be good as new. But I wanted to come across and let you know, so you didn't think I'd just disappeared and not made good on my promise."

"Oh," she said, hoping she wasn't blushing. "No, that's… well…"

"I mean, you can still have it, but it might be toward the end of the weekend? If that's too long for you, I'll gladly point you in the right direction to the antique shops I mentioned earlier. But, like I say, I don't know what you'll end up finding in there."

Jannie watched him as he paused and took a swig of his beer. It was clear he was apologetic for the mess up, but he wasn't, in any way, nervous, which made her feel more at ease too.

"Sure," she said. "I mean, that would be great, as long as you don't mind… if it's too much trouble then…"

"It's no trouble," he said as his eyes traveled to the step ladder that was running up and out of sight onto the mezzanine floor above. "Is that where it's going?" he asked as he nodded in the same direction.

"Yes," she said. "It's a good space up there. Perfect to use as an office."

"And how long are you staying?" he said, his eyes fixing on her again.

"I've leased for six weeks," she said between sips of her wine. "But I have the option to stay longer... if I need to."

He nodded and took another swig of his beer. His eyes were fixed on her and she found herself wanting to step closer. He was so handsome, and his presence in the room was dominating. The cabin was small, and he seemed to take up half of the living area. He was so tall and muscular, his shoulders were so broad, and he had an air of such great confidence about him that it was endearing.

His energy was overpowering, and it made her heart thump harder.

"Okay," he said. "It shouldn't be a problem getting it up there. Even if I have to tie something around it and hoist it up from above."

Jannie watched him stride to the ladder and begin to climb. He did it so fluidly and with such ease that it was as if he had some kind of extreme power. At the top rung, he stopped and looked around at the space.

"It'll be fine," he said, before he turned and climbed down, two steps at a time. "Nice space, you're right."

Jannie chuckled and shrugged her shoulders.

"I don't know a whole lot about interiors, but that space was one of the things that sold this place for me."

"I can imagine," he said. "Where you from?"

"Closer to the west coast," she said. "Small town, not too different to this, just a more pacific setting."

He smiled at her and they were locking eyes again. Her butterflies were flapping their wings and churning her belly into a nervous wreck. But it felt good. It was certainly a surprise to have been distracted like that.

"Well," he sighed as he looked at Jet who was waiting

patiently for him by the doorway. "It's that time of night where I take Jet for a wander into town and sink a few beers."

She smiled and scratched the side of her neck.

"Have you been into town?" he asked her.

She shook her head. "Only this morning on my way through, but I didn't really stop."

"Do you know all the good places to go?"

"I don't know anywhere to go," she admitted.

Dash chewed his bottom lip and looked at her as if he were sizing her up.

"Well, you can tag along if you like," he said teasingly. "As long as you promise not to cause any trouble."

Jannie's optimism bubbled radiantly inside her chest, and she knew her eyes would be glistening. Hell, she couldn't think of anything she would rather do than head off into town with this guy. But it was her first night in town, and she didn't want to cling to one person so soon. There was plenty she could be doing back at the cabin… sorting through her things, checking over her research… staying the hell away from bad boys! But… the offer was tempting.

He raised his eyebrows and his shoulders as if he were waiting for her reply.

"I mean, I shouldn't, but…" she said.

He raised the bottle to his lips and drained the rest of his beer. Jannie sensed he was about to turn and walk to the door, so she knew she had to make a quick decision. Her head was screaming at her, telling her to stay put for the night, but the devil on her shoulder was telling her to embrace the new experience and go out and have fun. She may not get an offer like this again, and who knew who she may meet once she was in town. Plus, it's not like she was complaining about having to spend time with Dash. He was all kinds of sexy.

"Okay," she said, "I'd love to."

She reached to the stool at the kitchen island and grabbed her purse, and as they headed to the front door, she drained the rest of her glass and grabbed her jacket from the hook in the hallway.

"Come on then, Jannie," Dash said as he stepped out into the crisp early evening air. "Let me show you the real Bridge Hollow."

CHAPTER 5

As they walked through Main Street, Dash clamped a cigarette between his teeth and lit it with a flick of a lighter. There was something about him that was effortlessly cool, and although it made him all the more attractive, it also scared the hell out of Jannie.

She had known his type before. Dangerous men only ever led to heartache, and not only that; they were usually only after one thing and they never truly cared about the women they were messing with. Dylan had been like that. He had been a total smooth criminal when it had come to wooing her, but the second he had her where he wanted her, he had done his best to tear her apart.

Jannie wouldn't go down that road again. And it didn't matter how handsome Dash was, or any other man she met for that matter, she knew she had to put her sanity first. She wasn't prepared to be walked all over again. If she was ever going to date, she wanted it to be someone who cared for her and protected her. Not exploited her in any way they could.

They wandered past a small park that seemed to be right in the center of town, and Jannie noticed the statue that she had seen countless times on the internet and on television documentaries. The Bridge Hollow Bear.

She stopped and stared at it, and when Dash realized she was falling behind, he turned and looked at her.

Jannie had wondered about this statue for so long, and now that it was right there in front of her, it was an amazing sight to see. It was bigger than she had thought it would be. Much, much bigger. The bear was ripping out of a man's skin and the look of anguish on its face was raw. It was violent and the energy from it was evident even from a hundred feet away.

"Oh, *that...*" Dash said as he exhaled a plume of smoke into the air with a smirk. "That thing needs ripped down."

"Ripped down?" she asked, almost breathless. "But why?"

"It just gets the tourists all juiced up," he rolled his eyes. "Makes them far too excited about things that shouldn't concern them."

She felt her interest peak when he said this. She knew there was something different about Dash, but the way he was so strong and big, it was almost as if he were from another planet. Could it be that he was part of the magic that had been the stuff of legends around this town?

She narrowed her eyes and looked at him. She always thought, if she ever saw a shifter, she would know it the second she had. But she didn't get that feeling with Dash. She must be going mad.

She shook her head and rolled out her shoulders as if she were trying to physically banish the thought.

"Come on," Dash said. "That statue and the people who worship it are barking up the wrong tree."

He winked and then continued walking.

She followed behind him until she caught back up, and she watched as Jet trotted across the street and navigated his way through traffic effortlessly.

"Jet is really good at that," she said. "It's like he could predict the next car."

"I trained him well," Dash shrugged. "If you spend time with animals, you can really get to know them. Most people get pets and only scratch the surface. They don't really connect to their full potential. It's sad really."

Jannie nodded, although she didn't really know what he meant. She had never had a dog, or any pet, of her own. But she could see the bond they shared; it was deep and heart-warming to watch. Jet stopped in front of a wooden building, and Jannie felt her gut tighten as she saw the row of motor-cycles lined up outside. It was the kind of sight you would see on a dirty city street, not in the middle of a postcard picturesque town.

"What's that about?" she asked. "Do you have lots of bikers around here?"

Dash smirked.

"Not really," he said. "But there's a group that come here from another town. They're a gang called The Forsaken Riders, and they have an affiliation with some of the folks around here."

"The Forsaken Riders?" Jannie asked with a raised brow. "And are they actually bikers? Like *outlaws*?"

Dash looked at her and nodded his head with a cheeky smile. This was all clearly very amusing to him.

"Jeez," she said as she reached up and gripped the strap on her purse. "I didn't expect this town to be so... so..."

"So what?" Dash asked with flirtatious menace.

"I don't know... just so... dangerous ,I guess."

Dash laughed as he wrapped a friendly arm around her shoulder.

"Girl, seriously, you have no idea."

·   ·   ·

The bar Jet was waiting in front of had a sign above the door that read, SHIFTER'S BLISS. As they walked over the threshold, Jannie's excitement level began to heighten, and she looked at Dash in an even closer way as they moved through the crowd.

He was different than anyone she had met before. And now that she was looking at him properly, she was sure she could sense something animalistic about him. He had such a strong connection to Jet too… it was as if they had their own secret method of communication. What if Dash had told her all of that as a cover up, and really, he could understand Jet in a way that she never could. Maybe they spoke a similar language…

Her thoughts started to run away with her, and she had to internally scold herself, telling herself to stop. She didn't even know if any of the rumors about this town were true, and there was certainly no evidence in the wider world. But she liked to think of herself as open minded, and the stories her grandmother had told her had come directly from her grandfather, who had been to Bridge Hollow decades before and had come home with tales of magic.

The bar was dark and packed, as it was a Friday night. Dash moved through the throngs of people and headed to the main area, where servers were taking turns, behind the bar, serving up beers and spirits. They moved quickly and efficiently, and Jannie noticed when one of the guys who was serving nodded at Dash and Dash nodded back.

He stopped when he reached the counter and leaned over it, and Jannie slipped in beside him and tried not to look too nervous. It was a strange mix of people. There appeared to be plenty of tourists milling around, but there was also a sense of locals and tight groups that had formed in various parts of the room.

"Hey, Dash," the guy behind the bar said as he stepped up to them and looked over at Jannie.

She gave a weak smile and Dash took another drag on his cigarette.

"Ryder, this is Jannie, she's new to town. Leasing a place up on my lake."

"Well, hello, Jannie," Ryder smiled and held out his hand.

She reached out to take it, but Dash put his arm across the bar in front of her and intercepted their fingertips touching. Ryder looked at Dash sternly and the two seemed to pass a glance between them that said more than words ever could. The tension between them began to rise, and Ryder took a breath.

"Sorry dude," Ryder said genuinely, and then quickly straightened out and reached behind himself to the rows of refrigerators behind the counter. "Your usual?"

"Please." Dash smiled. "And what about you?" He looked at her with irritation, as if, suddenly, she was someone who had become a problem to him.

"Oh, I… umm…," she began as she tried to see what was on offer.

"She'll take a glass of red wine," he said with a shrug.

Jannie had to stop herself from laughing. He was so odd. He had gone from being completely normal to shutting her down in a matter of seconds. She hoped he wasn't trying to play the big man in front of his friends. And what was that weirdness over Ryder trying to shake her hand?

She felt her brow crease with confusion, but she realized she didn't have the energy. This night was turning out strange, and she decided she would finish her drink and then get herself home.

"Thanks," she said as Dash passed the large glass to her, smiling before nodding to the other side of the room.

"Come on," he said as he wandered over to a table in the corner and waited for her to sit down.

When she had made herself comfortable, she looked him in the eyes and shook her head.

"You didn't have to invite me here," she said. "And anyway, don't worry about babysitting me. I'm fine on my own, thanks for showing me the good place to go."

She turned herself slightly, so she was no longer looking in his direction, and started to move slightly to the beat of the music. She could see that a stage had been set up toward the back of the room and she wondered what kind of band would be coming on later.

"I'm not babysitting you," he half laughed. "Come on, no need to get all defensive."

Jannie looked back at him over her shoulder and shrugged.

"It's cool," she said, determined to let him off the hook and put an end to his weirdness. "I'm totally fine. I came to this town by myself and I don't need a chaperone. But thanks for showing me how to get here and for the drink."

She raised her glass and smiled warmly at him, and then turned her back to him fully and stared at the stage, waiting patiently for something to happen over there so she didn't feel so awkward.

Dash stayed sitting behind her and she could feel him moving around on the seat as if he were looking for something. When she felt his hand on her shoulder, she looked back at him and he was holding out a small, ratty piece of paper with a number scrawled on it.

"Look," he said, "things can sometimes get weird around here... if you need anything... just call me, okay?"

His look was sincere, and she reached out slowly to take it.

As she did, their fingertips brushed against each other's

and she felt a rush of electricity fire down her fingers, hands, wrists and right up her arms, directly into her heart. She gasped and felt completely stunned, and when she looked up and they locked eyes, she saw it for real this time... an intense green swirling around his pupil. It was electric and almost neon. It was something otherworldly.

"D... D... Dash...," she stammered, but he pulled his hand away, and the force between them seemed to disappear.

She took a deep breath and looked at her hand before she looked to him again, but he was gone. The space at the table where he had been sitting was completely empty and the crowd had surged even more in front of her; she couldn't see any way out, or any place he might be.

"What the hell...," she whispered as she looked down at the piece of paper he had given her and at the digits scrawled across it.

She didn't know what had just happened, but he had done something to her when their fingers had touched, and then he had run. Now, she was all alone in Shifter's Bliss, and she had never craved someone so much before. He was all she could think about, and all she knew she had to stay away from... or it could very well be her undoing.

CHAPTER 6

The sun rose over the forest and shone into the windows of her bedroom. Jannie lay on her back, still half asleep, and she stretched her arms up until she felt them click. It had been one of the best night's sleep she had ever had, and she was wanting to prolong it for as long as possible.

She had come home from the bar the previous evening and double locked the front door. Then, she had found herself sitting in the darkness, staring out the double doors and across the lake toward Dash's cabin. There had only been one light on in one of the top rooms, and there had been no sign of him or Jet, but she still couldn't help but watch the house. It made her feel almost safe to think of him over there.

She rolled onto her side and bunched the covers up around her. It had been a crazy first day in town, and she didn't really know what to make of it all. Firstly, she had met Dash and there had clearly been a spark between them. Then, he had acted strange the moment they had arrived at Shifter's Bliss. Her mind settled on the moment Ryder had gone to shake her hand. He had acted so bizarre, and the tension between them had been thick. But why was it such a big deal for her to shake another man's hand?

She sighed and finally forced herself to her feet. She scraped her hair back into a messy topknot and then she grabbed her robe and pulled it on, tying it around her waist. She walked slowly down the hallway to the kitchen and living area, and she instantly looked up at the windows and to Dash's house across the lake.

The water was completely still, but Jannie could see another family, out on their terrace to the right of her, and even though they were in the distance, it looked like they may have had two young boys with them.

"What a nice place to come with a family," she smiled.

It really was a lovely little lake, and she wondered what it must be like to live there all year round. Her eyes traveled back to Dash's, but there was still nothing to suggest that anyone was home. No lights shone out from the inside.

She turned back to her kitchen and put on some water to boil. She made herself a cup of tea and settled at the island with some of the research she had brought with her to town.

Over the past few years, she had been especially interested in the stories of shifters and the idea of men who could turn into animals or fantastical beasts. When she had searched online, she had found so many legends and stories of people who had had personal experiences, but the town of Bridge Hollow kept reappearing. Since she had been a child, her grandmother had told her tales of her grandfather's travels, and they always came back to the same town.

Bridge Hollow.

It was a place he had come to for work, when he was a young man, not long before the second World War, and he had found himself swept up in the legends and all the magic of the mountain. Her grandmother had always been slightly cagey when it came to exact details, but she had made it abundantly clear that her grandfather believed there was something special about this place. And he truly believed in the existence of shifters.

Jannie opened the folder on the table and scattered out the information in front of her. She had her own notes, pages upon pages of ideas, to do with weaving shifters into her book, and then she had newspaper articles and clippings from strange events that had happened and been connected to the town... and, in particular, the things that had been happening since the beginning of the year.

She looked at the article on the missing hunters, the weather and the way it had changed in this area, the trees and land that appeared to be rotting, and the animals and birds that seemed to have just collapsed and died. One thing she had noticed in all of them, was that it appeared to happen in the center of a forest, close to where an abandoned mine had been located. And it had sparked her interest.

Her grandmother had mentioned the mine. Her grandfather had been tied to it, in some way, all those years ago and he had told her stories about the theories and legends. Now that Jannie was there in town, she wondered if she would hear anything about it, or even if she would dare to go looking herself.

She flicked another page and looked at the image in front of her. It was of a man turning into a wolf and it made a tingle run down her spine. She looked at the notes she had highlighted on the printout and it was on shifter and animal behavior. She scanned down the article and began to read. As she made her way through it, things were beginning to stand out to her, and her suspicions about Dash suddenly didn't seem very outlandish after all...

. . .

THESE MEN ARE INCREDIBLY ANIMALISTIC IN NATURE... THEY ARE natural-born protectors and will do anything to ensure the safety of their chosen ones. There is a theory that, within the shifting community, one is always looking for their fated and one true mate. Once they have discovered this other half of their soul, they are said to know instantly and will do anything to keep another shifter from imprinting on them first. Sometimes, this can lead to inter-pack fighting and serious danger for all concerned...

JANNIE RUBBED THE BACK OF HER NECK AND THOUGHT OF THE way Dash had stopped Ryder from taking her hand. It wasn't exactly the biggest declaration of love and commitment, but it had definitely meant something. Something that Ryder had understood and hadn't questioned.

She bit the corner of her lip and felt herself get a little excited. Maybe she should write a book about a shifter boyfriend.

She grabbed her pen and started to write some notes as fast as she could before the ideas in her head all floated away.

AS THE DAY WORE ON, JANNIE HAD WRITTEN AT LEAST FIVE full pages of ideas and notes and all freehand. She sat back and exhaled, her wrist and hand aching as she pushed the papers all out across the table and looked at them. She had invented a world where the men protected their women, but she imagined them all to be emotionally immature and unavailable. She thought of the legends she had heard about these creatures, how their magic made them superior in so many ways, but their fear of being discovered had driven them deep underground. She could only imagine that, if they were to ever fall in love or get involved with a human woman, they wouldn't be the best kind of boyfriend. In fact, she had the feeling they would be a complete nightmare. She imagined their intense sexual energy, the fact that they would probably have groupies wanting to sleep with them. She wondered if Bridge Hollow ever got serious Shifter fans turning up, girls looking to get laid by a man who was half beast and enjoying the excitement of the danger attached to it.

Danger was something Jannie certainly didn't need.

It was her biggest fear.

She had been down that road so many times, and now she was determined to look after herself, and the more she thought about the precarious nature of the town, the more she wondered if she should even be there at all.

She looked around the delightful little kitchen, and the way it opened out into the gorgeous living area with the vaulted ceiling and mezzanine level above. She looked out across the lake, at the clear blue water, at the sky-high pine trees and the stunning views. She had heard this place was dangerous, and even Dash had said to her the night before that things could get weird around town... but she honestly couldn't see how, when she was sitting in such an tranquil location.

"How *wild* could things honestly get around here?" She laughed to herself as she looked at how peaceful the scenery was around her. "Maybe in town things can get a little hairy, especially with those burly looking bikers hanging around... but here, around this lake? I just don't see it..." She shrugged her shoulders and jumped down from the bar stool.

It was almost 4pm and she had spent a full day, dreaming up ideas and working. She missed not having a real designated writing area, but knew she was lucky to have Dash's help. She wondered when he would bring the desk over for her and help her get it set up on the mezzanine.

She looked down at the piece of paper on the table. She

had kept it close to her since the night before and even though she hadn't entered his number into her phone, the temptation to call him had been pulling at her since he had left her back at Shifter's Bliss.

She chewed her bottom lip and twiddled the paper in her hands. She had such a strong urge to call him, and her heart had been tingling ever since their fingertips had touched in the bar. He had done something to her, even if it was just awakening her to the possibility that she didn't really need to be celibate for the rest of her life. And now, she felt connected to him somehow… as if there was a pull between them. She looked back toward his cabin and noticed that Jet was out on the dock. It was as if he were lounging and looking her way. She wondered if dogs had better eyesight and if he could see her clearly, or whether she was just some kind of blur to him inside a window–that was, if he could even see her at all.

She noticed a sharp glint of blue, and even though he was far away, she could felt as if it had come from his eyes. She was sure she had seen it. As if Jet had heard her thoughts and it made her clutch her robe at her neck and take a step back.

She held her breath for a moment, until she was sure that she must have just been imagining it, and then she turned and headed back into the hallway and away from temptation.

She was going to get showered and dressed and walk back to town for an early dinner. It had been a long day alone, even with all her wonderful ideas flowing and her creativity peaking. But now, she was ready for a change of scenery, and she knew just where she wanted to go.

CHAPTER 7

*D*ash rubbed a sweaty palm down his face, grazing against his stubble and itching his skin. He had had a tough few days. In fact, he had had a tough year in general. Bridge Hollow had been all kinds of fucked up lately, and he and his pack knew something dangerous was about to happen.

They could smell it in the air. They could see it in the way the trees moved. The animals around them may have spoken a different language, but he knew they felt it. They all could.

And now, something had murdered a man right there in front of their eyes in the middle of Shifter's Bliss.

What the fuck was he going to do?

He, Ryder and the rest of their packs had taken the body of the drunk to the top of the mountain and buried him in a shallow grave. It was the first time that the bears and wolves had truly had to come together and do something that they would all swear an oath to protect. The man had been a Bridge Hollow resident. He had been missing now for almost a month and there were posters up around town. It had, so far, managed to stay clear of national and state news, but he and everyone else knew it was only because the town's sheriff was pacifying the family and giving them false hope.

The truth was, the sheriff was just as worried as the packs. He may not have known what he was up against, but he certainly could see strange things were happening and he didn't know what to do about it. Dash could see his fear of looking incompetent or in over his head was clouding his judgement, and for all of them, during this difficult time, that was probably for the best.

The puncture wounds on the victim's neck had suggested something particularly sinister. And they had known they could no longer face whatever was coming on their own. For years, the town's packs had stayed apart from each other. Wolves and bears had always trod a fine line, and after the initial unrest a few months ago, when they had all started to act crazy, they had known that they were going to have to come together, to join forces for the good of them all.

Dash picked up a cigarette and flicked a lighter. He inhaled and instantly felt calmer as the nicotine coursed through his veins. He knew he had to quit, he didn't even like it that much, but in stressful times his good habits seemed to be diminishing, and he knew he had to get back on track. But now, he had the added stress of the girl.

Jannie.

She was something else.

When he had seen her standing there on the dock on the opposite side of the lake, he had felt something come at him, fast and furious. It was like a rush on the wind, and it hit him full in the face and woke him up.

He hadn't been expecting it, and now, he was more confused than ever. She was someone to him... he felt it deeply. He had never looked at a human and wanted to be so close to them, but he couldn't pull her into all of this. He was glad she was only staying for six weeks. If it had been any longer, he honestly didn't know how he would cope. He had shot himself in the foot by offering to give her the desk because now, he was going to have to see her again. He had had to force himself away from her the night before when she had gone with him to Shifter's Bliss. She had tried to push him away in the same way, and he had tried to resist... but in the end, his common sense had taken over.

He couldn't get involved with *anyone* right now. Especially, a human. And especially, someone he thought could be the one he was waiting for. With that being said, he still didn't want another shifter even shaking her hand. He wasn't taking any chances that anyone else could develop a bond with her. He wanted her all to himself.

And that was where his head was fucked.

He knew he wanted her.

He knew he needed her.

He even knew that he felt things that he never thought he ever would... but, with the unrest in Bridge Hollow, he was scared.

Scared that this perfect girl could get hurt.

Scared that he could put her in harm's way.

And scared that, with this all happening around him, he may not be able to protect her in the way he deeply needed to.

He took another drag on his cigarette.

This was all so fucked.

"Hey!" Ryder's voice came from behind him and broke his thoughts, and he turned to see him standing in the doorway of the bar.

"Hey," Dash exhaled.

He had been waiting for him, and now that he was here, it was time for them to go and find advice from an elder. A shifter that none of them had seen or made contact with for decades.

They knew he lived up on the mountain, set away from prying eyes and well above where the skiers liked to go. It was off the main track and away from the slopes and routes that the tourists tended to take. It was cloaked in magic, a place that not even Dash had ever seen.

This elder was a shifter dragon.

And now they were going to find him and ask for his advice. He was the only one they could turn to.

"Are you ready?" he asked Ryder who sidled up beside him and exhaled deeply through his nose.

"I don't know," Ryder said. "But I guess we've got no choice."

Dash nodded and threw his smoking cigarette on the ground and stomped it out with his boot.

"Let's go," Dash said as he moved forward, and they started to walk in the direction of the base of the mountain. "Once we're in the trees, we can shift and run."

"Sounds good to me," Ryder smirked as they continued to stride.

They were now two men on a mission.

They had to find out what was happening in town. Because not only did they have Bridge Hollow to protect, but now, Dash had something else he wanted to protect to.

Jannie.

This girl was important.

CHAPTER 8

Jannie looked at herself in the mirror and smiled. She was in love with her new outfit and she felt perfectly mountain chic. She had put together a pair of skinny jeans with long black knee boots, a black turtleneck and a grey faux-fur gilet. Her dark hair was long and wavy, down over her shoulders and she had spent some time painting her nails a rich purple, which was something she rarely did.

She had had such a positive day; she had worked her ass off on her writing, relaxed and did some yoga overlooking the lake, and now she was showered and ready to head out for an evening meal.

It had been two days since she had seen Dash. And now, she was wondering if she would ever see him again. The cabin on the other side of the lake had remained dark. Jet had been in and out on various occasions, but generally, she hadn't seen any other movement or signs of life. And now she was worried if he was avoiding her.

He had given her his number, but there was no way she was texting or calling him. He knew exactly where she was, and if he wanted to see her, or the desk was ready, then he knew what to do.

She wasn't going to be the one doing any sort of chasing. Especially, after a guy who smoked, looked badass and was covered in tattoos.

She kept reminding herself that he was trouble with a capital T.

She was safer on her own. Safer concentrating on her work and safer enjoying her own company and personal growth.

Dash would only distract her and get her in trouble. She was sure of it.

She grabbed her handbag and she headed to the main door of the cabin. After she had exited and locked it behind her, she started to walk up and out of the little dip that kept the lake hidden amongst the trees.

Now that she had been in town for a few days, she was used to the walk. After the first night, when Dash had taken her with Jet, she had done it each day since. She would be lying if she said she hadn't been hoping to bump into him at some point, but she had been actively avoiding Shifter's Bliss, just in case he was there, making it seem as if she were looking for him.

She had tried a couple of the coffee houses in town and one of the fancier restaurants that had been full of tourists. It was a quaint little Italian place, but it was lit by candles and all the tables had white clothes and linen. It had reminded her of some of the family run places she visited back home, old school and traditional in their atmosphere, but the food had been hearty and satisfying.

She had barely eaten all day and her stomach was beginning to rumble. She had decided that while she was away and concentrating on her selfcare and personal growth, this would be the perfect time to try and cut out bread and not overindulge. But obviously, since she had done that, bread had been all she could think about and she craved it like crazy. All she wanted was a cheeseburger, something big and greasy, with fries and a diet coke.

Selfcare at its finest!

She smirked to herself as she wandered along the mountain road and began to approach town. She enjoyed her evening walks the most as they gave her the opportunity to watch the sun set over the lakes and the mountains as she went. It made her feel alive and connected to nature, and it also meant that she could try and figure out which part of the forest this legendary mine could potentially be located.

As she approached Main Street, she slowed her pace and enjoyed walking among the tourists and the residents of the town. It really was so lovely there, and the evenings really seemed to make the whole place come alive. As she passed by the Bridge Hollow Bear in the center of town, she stopped for a moment and looked at it. It really was magnificent, and she saw a collection of tourists taking turns to stand in front of it and have their photographs taken.

She reached into her purse and pulled out her cellphone and took a quick snap of it herself, even with the tourists around it, and then she made a mental note to make sure she checked it out on her way back to the cabin later to try and get a proper picture for her collection.

She had her notebook in her bag, and she was ready to pass the time while she was having dinner writing and jotting down more notes and ideas. She truly had been awakened and her creativity was sparking. Bridge Hollow was certainly good for her soul.

She took a slight turn and crossed over onto the other side of Main Street and as she did, she suddenly felt a familiar presence close by her. She didn't know how she could tell that it was him, but her heart instantly began to beat harder and a tingle seemed to crawl all over her, as if her body was responding to his, and her skin was radiating heat to try and attract him.

She stopped and didn't dare move.

Was she actually going mad?

What on earth was this sensation rippling through her?

She reached up and touched her chest and she could feel the heat beneath her clothes. Her skin was burning hot, but it wasn't distressing her. It wasn't a fever. It was a lovely warm glow making her feel as if she would be shining with energy.

She took a deep breath and prepared herself to turn around. As she did, she made sure she did it slowly, and when she saw Dash standing there ahead of her, his piercing green eyes fixed on her and his stunningly dark features popping out and catching her there like a fly in a web, she couldn't help but smile.

She had felt him before she had seen him, and from the glinting green in his eyes, she knew now that she wasn't going mad at all.

Dash was a shifter.

He had to be.

He oozed his animalistic nature and she could almost feel the power emanating from him.

The green glinted across his eyes again—they shone brightly—and he took a step closer to her. He held out his hand, and even though they were at least ten feet apart, she felt his energy pulling her to him.

She moved and let her hand move up and take his. When their fingers connected this time, it was stronger than before. Their souls and their energies mixed together, they intertwined and the heat between them was so strong and powerful, it made her knees shake.

"Dash…," she whispered, her eyes fixed on his, unable to tear herself away.

He didn't say a word, but he took a step closer to her and their bodies were almost fully touching.

She barely dared breathe, and she couldn't speak.

Dash reached up and brushed a strand of hair behind her ear and his eyes were glistening with color and power.

"I'm sorry, Jannie," he whispered. "I don't want you to get hurt…"

As he said the words, she felt her walls trying to spring up. She wanted to push him away, but she could see the pain in his eyes.

"I'm so drawn to you," he whispered. "But is isn't safe here…"

"What do you mean?" she asked with a slight sense of panic.

She could see from the look in his eyes that he was afraid for her. She had thought that if he were a shifter, he would be emotionally immature and unavailable, but from the way he was acting, she was beginning to think she must have gotten it wrong.

This man was clearly solid, and he was having trouble with his feelings. He clearly had a strong sensation when they were together, just like she had.

"We need to talk," he whispered.

"Okay," she said, her eyes still fixed on his.

They were holding each other in place, in the center of town, and in those moments, it was as if there was no one else around. Their lips could only have been centimeters from each other, and she could feel the heat from his hand cupping her face. Whatever he was doing to her was changing her from the inside out. But she didn't want to run from it this time, it felt right. It was as if this was exactly where she was supposed to be.

He let his big, rough hand fall away from her face and it took hold of hers. He smiled at her and she felt something even deeper, something real and true, as if they had known each other since the beginning of time.

"Are you hungry?" he asked her, a glint passing over his green eyes.

"Starving," she grinned.

He squeezed her hand tightly and pulled her along as he began to move further down Main Street.

"Come on," he said. "I know just the place."

CHAPTER 9

She had been expecting him to make the turn into Shifter's Bliss, but Dash had strolled on by, still gripping her hand tightly and walking with her as if they had done this a thousand times.

It was strange for her to see him this way—he was determined and taking charge; she hadn't been able to tell that he had it in him, but he had kept her at such a distance. Now that he was letting her in and coming closer to her, it was as if she were seeing the real Dash for the first time.

He slowed his pace when he reached a little diner on a road that intersected Main Street. It looked shabby and old, but completely authentic, and the smell of the food that was drifting out to meet them on the pavement was driving her wild.

"My god," she said, "that smells so good."

Dash smiled.

"It's one of the best," he said. "Wait until you see the menu."

He held the door open for her to walk through ahead of him. When she looked up and around at the wonderful décor, she couldn't believe she had walked by this place so many times and not given it a second thought.

It wasn't just the menu that was wonderful, because the décor was too. It was old and rustic, all wooden tables with red and white checked tablecloths, antlers mounted on the walls and neon lights. She could hear the sizzle of the grill back in the kitchen, the music was just low enough for it not to be overpowering, and the men and women in there were clearly more local than they were tourists.

"One of town's best kept secrets," he winked. "For some reason, the tourists don't seem interested in this place… but we all know better."

"Hey, Dash!" A waitress smiled as she stepped over with a pencil behind her ear.

Jannie looked at her nametag and noted that it said, *Emily*. She looked young, maybe twenty at most, and she had blonde hair–perfectly braided and long–right down her back. She was pretty and almost cherubic in appearance, and it was clear that they must have known each other well. She seemed completely at ease around him.

"Hey, Em," he said. "You got a booth for two?"

"Sure thing," she said as she grabbed a couple menus and started to walk toward the back of the room.

She stood next to a corner booth and smiled as they climbed inside and then she laid the menus down.

"Can I get you something to drink?" she asked.

Dash looked across at Jannie and she shrugged.

"I'm going to have a beer," he smiled.

"Of course," Jannie teased. "Well, I guess, I'll have a beer too then."

Dash cocked his head to the side and gave her an impressed smile. Emily moved away from the table to get them their drinks from the bar, and Jannie wiggled her eyebrows.

"I didn't think you'd be the beer kind of girl," Dash said warmly.

"There's a lot you don't know about me," she said confidently. "And by the looks of things, there's plenty I don't know about you either."

Dash leaned forward and his eyes glinted again.

"I get the feeling you know more than you let on..." he whispered.

Jannie's heart was pounding out of her chest. She was so into him, and seeing him again, after two days of being denied, was rousing feelings that she didn't know were possible.

"Maybe," she said as she grinned and bit her lip. "But I want you to tell me... what is going on?"

He looked up as Emily approached the table and set down two beers. Jannie and Dash thanked her, and then she moved away as they pretended to look at the menus.

"I don't want Emily to hear any of this," he said quietly, as a way of explanation. "I've known her since she was a kid. She's a friend of mine from high school's younger sister, and she certainly isn't as *in the know* as even you appear to be."

"In the know?" Jannie asked with a raised eyebrow.

"I get the feeling you sense something in me," he said. "I've known it since the second I first saw you. And when you said you were a writer, I don't know... I got the feeling you were here to cover a news story. Maybe something to do with our legends and our past..."

"I'm not a journalist," she told him firmly. "I did tell you that when you asked the first time."

He smiled at her warmly; he clearly enjoyed her feistiness.

"Well, I'm glad," he said. "Because the people around here, they don't like being investigated."

"Which people?" she asked as she leaned forward.

Dash took a sip of his beer but his eyes never left hers.

"What have you heard about Bridge Hollow?" he asked her.

Jannie swallowed and bit her bottom lip. She had no idea what was going to happen when she told him she was a believer, but she just hoped it wouldn't push him away.

"I don't know much," she whispered. "But I know what you are."

His eyebrows raised slightly, but then he smiled and nodded his head.

"Okay," he said. "Were you looking for that when you came here?" He seemed serious.

"No," she told him honestly. "I came here for inspiration for a book I want to write. I didn't know what I believed... but I had heard plenty of stories... and then, when I met you, I don't know. I was confused at first, I didn't get the feeling that you were a..." she mouthed the word, *shifter*. "I had read things about them, and I thought that I would know straight away if I ever met one... but it wasn't until our fingers touched and something happened... something big."

He nodded his head slowly.

"Something big did happen," he confirmed. "Something that even I wasn't expecting."

She swallowed nervously, and he reached out and took hold of her hands. When she felt his warmth, she was comforted, and she liked what she was feeling.

"I didn't mean for this to happen," he whispered. "I don't want to drag you into something that is going to be dangerous... but fate doesn't take any prisoners."

"Fate..." she whispered.

The word was so apt. It was as if they had been waiting their whole lives to be led to this point, to be sat opposite each other right here in this diner, to be holding hands and to be looking into each other's eyes.

"I don't want any danger," she said. "But when I'm with you, for some reason, that all seems to go out of the window."

She was so confused. She knew she shouldn't be walking headfirst into something risky, but for Dash, it all seemed to be worth it. She just hoped she wasn't going to get burned.

"What is going on here in this town?" she asked him.

Dash took a deep breath and then he tapped the menu.

"Emily is coming back over," he said. "Let's order and then we can really talk."

"Okay," Jannie agreed.

She felt a twist of dread knot in her stomach and she suddenly she felt way out of her depth again.

Whatever he was about to tell her, she knew it wasn't going to be good.

"A few weeks before you came to town, someone was murdered in Shifter's Bliss," Dash said before he took a big bite of his burger.

"What?" Jannie's eyes had grown wide and she couldn't believe what she was hearing.

They had waited until their food had arrived and they knew they weren't going to be disturbed anymore. The tables around them had cleared out, and they had the back of the restaurant to themselves, and it was clear that Dash was feeling more comfortable about talking now that they were all alone.

"A man, a drunk," he said sadly. "He was a resident of the town, and somebody that everyone kind of knew in one way or another. A familiar face I guess you could say."

"Okay…" Jannie urged him to continue, her heart raging in her chest.

"It happened in full view of everyone," he said. "And no one saw a thing."

He shook his head and took a swig of his beer.

"Things like that just don't happen here," he said with concern. "Me and my pack, we could sense danger in a room in a split second, but this guy had been lying dead for at least ten minutes... and he was cold. Ice cold."

Jannie felt a chill creep right up her spine.

"That's awful," she said.

"You must have heard, on the news, some of the stories that have been coming out here lately?" he said. "Plenty of people come here looking for the supernatural, but they don't truly believe it... What makes you different?"

Jannie sat back and looked at him. How could she explain that she just knew?

"I guess it must go back to my grandfather," she said. "He stayed here for a while, sometime around the second World War... He believed, and he told my grandmother stories and she passed them on to me. He was here and he had something to do with the mine... there's a mine here, right?"

Dash's face tightened and concern flashed all over it.

"What do you know about the mine?" There was a chill in his voice.

"Not a whole lot, really, just that my grandfather worked there, or he had something to do with it at one point. I'm not sure of the details."

"And he left town?" Dash asked with wide eyes.

"He was only here for six weeks...," she trailed off. "Kind of like I am."

Dash's eyes started to dart from one corner of the table to the other as he looked down at it with worry. Jannie could sense the panic in him, but he was also churning something over deep in his mind, as if he were debating telling her something but didn't know if he should.

"Promise me," he said as he finally looked up and their

eyes zoned in on each other's. "Promise me you won't go looking for it."

She was taken aback when he said the words. It was not what she had been expecting.

"You want me to promise you that I won't go looking for the mine?" she asked him.

He nodded.

She leaned back and felt nerves mounting inside of her.

Seriously, what the hell was she doing? This went against all she had promised herself.

"Okay," she said genuinely. "I promise I won't go looking for it. But why?"

Dash's eyes were on hers again and he held her hand across the table.

"I can't tell you," he said sternly. "But I need you to trust me."

Jannie was feeling more wary by the second, but she nodded her head. She didn't want to argue with him, and now that she had confirmation that he was what she thought he was, she didn't want to put herself in any more danger.

"If you can't tell me that," she said nervously, "can you at least tell me what you did to me when our hands touched back at the bar?"

Dash smiled warmly and gave her hand a little squeeze. The energy between them was electric and his heat was warming her right down to her bones.

"My kind all have one true mate," he said.

Her heart began to flutter. She remembered what she had read during her research only a couple days before.

"I don't want to scare you… but I think you're mine…"

He smiled, and Jannie felt as if the world had stopped spinning on its axis. The two of them could have been the only two people alive. Everything around them seemed to fall away, and all she could see was him.

Dash.

This incredible magical man, who had powers she didn't even truly understand.

"And what are you? A bear?" she whispered.

"I'm a wolf, Jannie," he said, his eyes tingling with green. "I'm a shifter wolf."

A wolf.

Jannie smiled and rested her other hand on top of his.

This badass wolf man was trying to claim her. And she had never been more excited or afraid.

CHAPTER 10

As they walked back to the lake in the dark, Dash kept his arm protectively around Jannie's shoulder. The temperature had dropped with the autumn sun, and the chill in the air was biting and harsh.

They walked under the canopy of pine trees, and in the middle of the branches, high above, the sky was clear and covered with stars. It had been a long time since Jannie had truly looked up at the moon and the heavens, but to see it there, all clear and sparkling, was a magic all its own.

Dash had been a complete gentleman, and he certainly hadn't put any moves on her just yet. The chemistry was so powerful between them, it was as if she had known him for a thousand years. She understood him deeply and without question, and she could tell that he felt the same.

The whole idea was crazy, and she didn't know how she was ever going to reason with herself over it, but she had often heard people say that when they met the person they were supposed to be with, *they just knew*.

This is exactly how she felt... and she was struggling to keep her hands off him.

They started to walk down the slope that led to Jannie's cabin, and she could feel that Dash was on alert. The darkness had really come in, and she could barely see a foot in front of her, but Dash strolled forward confidently and led her safely to her front door.

When she reached it, she turned and looked up at him. He was so handsome and sexy, and all she wanted to do was grab hold of him, kiss him and pull him inside with her. But she was still too afraid.

He traced a finger down her cheek and across her jawline, and she reached out and put her hands on his waist. She could feel how taught and muscular he was underneath his t-shirt, and the scent of cologne mixed in with smoke and beer was making her pussy ache. He was so much of a man. And she could see his protective side really coming forward. He really cared about her; she could feel it.

She smiled at him coyly and stared into his eyes, and when his hand went back up to her neck and took hold of her, her knees began to go weak.

When their lips met, it was as if an explosion were firing between them. His mouth opened and their tongues slipped up against each other's as they explored one another. Jannie's breath was taken away, her heart pounded hard and her whole body was tingling with desire and anticipation.

God, she wanted him.

She wanted him so badly she didn't know how she was going to be able to walk away from him and see him head around to his side of the lake. But she had to be strong.

She pushed herself against him and gripped his waist tightly, the heat between them getting stronger, and she could feel his desire growing into something she had never experienced before. Something powerful and animalistic.

Her pussy throbbed and her nipples hardened. She wanted so badly to wrap her legs around him and let him do things to her that she had promised herself she didn't need. She had promised herself she would sacrifice all her desires to save her heart, but the truth was, when she was with Dash, it was impossible. It didn't turn into a want... it was a deep need.

She needed him.

Her body craved him and responded to him in such an incredible way she didn't know how she would ever be the same again.

Their lips broke apart and she could barely breathe. Dash was panting and clearly getting hot and bothered, his eyes were shining a bright green in the darkness. He pulled his hand away and took a step back.

"Jannie," he panted, "I... I should go."

She nodded and pressed her back against the door.

She didn't want him to leave, but she knew she had a lot to weigh up. If she took this any further, then she was walking into a lot of danger, something she had promised herself she wouldn't do.

She had a lot to think about.

Dash began to back away from the cabin, and when he was far enough away but still facing and watching her, she slipped her key into the door, opened it and stepped inside.

She knew he was still waiting out there to make sure she was safe, and she was glad for it. To know she had a man like him watching over her was reassuring and it made her feel truly loved.

She walked through the cabin to the back quickly and sat in the darkness. She waited and waited until she saw a little light spring on in Dash's cabin across the lake thirty minutes later, and then she hugged her knees against her chest and imagined him stepping into his bedroom, taking off his leather jacket and t-shirt, and walking around with his incredible muscles on show.

How she wished she could touch them.

She bit her lip and rose slowly to her feet.

She had gotten herself in a right mess now.

Because she didn't know how she was ever going to be able to walk away.

THE LAKE WAS SHINING CRYSTAL CLEAR UNDERNEATH THE SUN and there was a light breeze in the air. She was sure she could hear music drifting down from the mountain; there was something peaceful and magical all around her.

She laid back on the grass and let the sun warm through her, her bikini the only thing she was wearing, as her back and thighs moved against the softness beneath her.

Her heart was already beating quickly, and she could feel his eyes on her from somewhere within the woods. She laid there for him, she wanted him to come for her.

She arched her back and moaned slightly, her whole body aching for his touch.

She heard the growls first, but she wasn't afraid. She knew she was being tracked by the wolf, and she wanted it to find her.

"Dash...," she whispered as she kept her eyes closed and pinned herself to the ground.

She opened her legs as she felt him coming closer, and when she felt his shadow cross over her, she finally opened her eyes to see him standing there, already completely naked, with only her in his sights.

Her breathing became more rapid and she opened her legs wider. She needed him inside of her. She couldn't wait any longer.

"Dash," she said again as he got down on his knees and crawled on top of her.

She let her hands finally touch him, at the heat emanating

from his incredible body. His physique was so strong and powerful, she knew he could dominate her and take charge, and she had never wanted it to happen more. He kissed her neck, her nipples hardened even more, and she wrapped her legs around him. The sun beat down on them from overhead, and each time he kissed her, a growl escaped his lips.

"I want you," he snarled as he pushed himself onto her.

She felt the heavy poke of his cock and it made her moan. She was soaking wet and so ready for him she didn't know how she could stand not to have him any longer.

She scraped her nails down his back, and he let out a howl of pleasure. A howl so deep and strong it sent a shiver right through her.

He was her wolf.

And she was his human.

She wanted him and needed him, and she was never going to walk away from him now.

She tipped her head up to meet his and kissed him deeply on the lips. Their passion was growing, and she was aching for him, her body wanted him so very badly that everything around her was becoming more fevered and frantic.

As she reached down, ready to take hold of his manhood and guide it into her, she was so overcome with anticipation that she gasped, and the sensation shot her back into the waking world...

She sat bold upright in bed, panting and gasping, her whole body turned on and aching for a man that wasn't there.

"No!" she cried as she slumped back down against the pillows and buried her head.

It had all been a dream.

An incredible dream... but a dream, nonetheless.

She and Dash had been about to consummate their love, but it had been cruelly ripped away from her.

She huffed and rolled over and clamped her eyes closed.

That dream had only confirmed to her what she was already afraid of.

Dangerous Dash and the wolf inside him had gotten into her head, and now she was hooked.

It didn't matter how much she tried to resist... he was right.

She was his.

CHAPTER 11

The forest was dark on the mountain and as Dash strolled through it with the rest of his pack, he had the feeling that this meeting was going to cause so much more trouble.

He had resisted the urge to turn since Jannie had come to town, but now that he was out in the wide open spaces and headed toward the place where the old abandoned mine lay, he had the overwhelming need to unleash the animal in him.

Some of the pack had already changed, and the wolves were running fast and free up ahead. They sniffed the ground and howled up at the moon above, and Dash felt the call inside of him growing stronger.

He let the heat wash over him and then he growled and howled as the energy ripped through him. The wolf began to tear through his skin, his clothes ripped clean away as the fur and ferociousness sprang free. As his arms and legs elongated, his nose lengthened and his eyes turned the brightest green, he felt a power that he had missed.

He had missed his inner animal. It was such a strong part of him, he didn't want to subdue it any longer.

His wolf stood tall and proud, and when he sniffed the air, he could sense the danger all around the forest. The mountain and the town of Bridge Hollow was no longer safe, and that meant that Jannie wasn't safe either.

He had to do this, he had to go to this meeting with the elder dragon and let his pack know what was truly coming their way.

They all ran on up the mountain, deeper into the forest and past the place of the abandoned mine that was now proving to be so much more of an issue than they had originally thought.

When they reached a clearing in the forest and the mountain evened out, they were aware that they were in a place that had long been forgotten. The elder dragon had hidden high above Bridge Hollow to save himself and his small clan. He didn't want the legends reaching them there and for people to come asking questions. A wolf out in the woods was one thing… but a dragon? He was never going to be safe amongst people. He was in danger and he knew it.

Dash stopped, and he and his pack stood in a line. The wolves were all together and ready to delve further. He had warned them what they were heading to, and he had also assured them that the elder dragon was on their side. He wanted to put an end to all the madness in Bridge Hollow as much as they did. He just needed them to hear him out.

The clearing was large and in the middle were two cabins nestled within the trees. Dash waited for the elder to come out; he knew they were there, he could sense their eyes on him and his pack.

Dash shifted back to his human form and urged the others to do the same. They stood there and waited until the door of the cabin creaked open and the old man emerged.

He looked broken and crooked, but Dash had seen this man around town many years before he had come up here and hidden away. And from his own family, he knew the legends about the dragon clan. They were hundreds of years old and full of magic. Now they were all joining together to defeat a powerful evil.

"Bishop...," Dash said as the old man made his way forward.

His own pack was clearly on edge, although the wolves knew deep down that they had to stay calm.

"Hello, Dash," the old man said.

Dash smiled and then he turned to look at his pack.

"I need you to tell them what you told me," he said sternly. "Before we can move forward and understand what we are dealing with."

Bishop sighed and stepped closer. Behind him, in the houses, Dash was sure he could see the eyes of other dragons, other men with magic in their veins, and ones who had been told to stay away and not get involved.

Dash understood their hesitation but also, it made him angry with them. They got to hide up there on the mountain with all their wisdom while the other packs down in town had to suffer and handle all the trouble themselves.

"You said a man was killed," Bishop said with a shaking voice. "Well, I think I know what did it... from the information you gave to me."

Dash looked at the other members of his pack and saw the way their eyes all seemed to light up.

"You know who killed the guy in Shifter's Bliss?" Maddox, Dash's second-in-command, asked.

Bishop nodded his head slowly and then cleared his throat.

"We have lived up here for decades now, in fear of being discovered," he began. "It would be easy to explain a wolf or bear being seen in the woods, but for a dragon to be seen by human eyes, it would cause us no end of trouble."

The shifters all nodded in agreement.

"There are other things that have found their way onto this mountain… things that arrived with the collapse of the mine and things that have long stayed buried…"

Dash felt his nerves rising.

"When the mind collapsed all those years ago, way back before any of you were born… it brought with it immense danger."

The wolves began to whisper amongst themselves, and Dash hushed them.

"As dragons are the oldest living shifters here in Bridge Hollow, we know what happened."

Dash stared at him, willing for him to continue.

"When the mine collapsed, it opened something… something bad… it let in our world, the shifter world, but it also let in something else."

"What do you mean?" Maddox asked.

"It pierced a veil between two worlds," Bishop continued. "Us dragons and the beginnings of your packs arrived here in Bridge Hollow, we came to this dimension… but other things, bad things, managed to escape with us."

"What kind of things?" one of the other wolves asked.

"Dangerous things…," he whispered.

"The thing that killed the guy in the bar?" Maddox asked.

Bishop nodded.

"Probably," he said. "For years, we have protected the mine, it's one of the reasons we are up here, and for so long, nothing terrible managed to work its way through. Bridge Hollow has always had its legends, and people who believe had long been drawn here… but we managed to ensure that nothing dark escaped… until now…"

Dash felt his blood run cold. He knew the severity of the situation now and he was truly afraid for his family, both his shifter brothers and the other people he loved.

"We think a vampire managed to get through," Bishop said sternly. "We have been keeping them at bay since the mine collapsed... them and other things... but somehow, since the beginning of the year, they seem to have found a way in."

"Jesus," Maddox gasped.

They had all known there was more to Bridge Hollow than had met the eye, and with them all being shifter packs, they had known they were part of the magic. But never in their wildest dreams could they have ever thought there was more waiting in the wings... A terrible danger ready to invade their world and take away everything they held dear.

"And where is this vampire now?" Dash asked. It was one of the only answers he hadn't managed to get from Bishop when he and Ryder had initially come to the mountain several days ago.

"We don't know," said Bishop. "He may have gone back through the veil, or he may still be here. All we know is we can't let anyone from town go anywhere near that mine."

All the wolves looked at each other and nodded. At last, something they were all in agreement on.

"Some of us love the people down there as if they were our own," Bishop said. "We need to make sure they are safe and kept out of harm's way... Meanwhile, we need hunting parties to look for this thing... and the place he may have managed to get through to our world."

"Do you think they've found another portal to here, away from the mine?" Maddox asked.

"We just don't know," said Bishop. "All we know is that whatever is coming into our world from that veil is killing our land and our animals... It made two hunters disappear and now, one of their creatures has broken through and killed a man in plain sight in the middle of town."

They could all sense the panic in his voice. This elder

dragon and his clan had been protecting Bridge Hollow from afar for a hundred years, and now their good work had been compromised. Somehow, the other side had found a way to get through.

"Okay," Maddox said sternly as he looked at Dash. "Well, we know what we need to do."

Bishop nodded.

"We need to arrange hunting parties to go out and find this thing," Dash said. "And we need the bears to help us too."

Bishop smiled and nodded.

"We are the good magic here," he said warmly. "It is time we all unite to defeat the bad."

He held out his hand, and all the wolves stood forward and did the same. They placed their hands together in the center of the circle and bumped their fists up against each other's.

When the meeting was over and Bishop had gone back to his cabin, Dash led his pack back down the mountain.

"We really are fucked, aren't we?" Maddox asked him as he ran a hand through his hair.

"We just need to come together and be strong," said Dash. "We don't truly know what we are up against, but we know it started at the mine, so I would like to think that will be the way to end it."

He strolled forward, and he didn't want to look back. He was glad he had taken advice from the elder dragon and was annoyed with himself for not asking sooner, as the answers had been there all along.

The magic of Bridge Hollow, the woods and the mountains around it, was about to explode with who knew what. If it had been a vampire that had managed to get through, then that meant more could follow... and with them, they could well bring about the end of humanity.

It was a terrifying thought... and now Dash also had

Jannie to think about. The human girl he was falling in love with and didn't want to be away from for one second more.

As he left the woods and slinked back to his cabin under the cloak of darkness, he knew he couldn't keep himself away from her any longer. So much was coming, and he had a long road ahead, but for now, he was determined to try to spend a few normal days with her. He was going to ask her out properly, take her the desk, and act as natural as possible so as not to worry her.

She was going to be worth the fear, he knew it.

She was something he never wanted, but something that had found him anyway. And he wasn't about to turn away from fate… that was something only a fool could do.

Jannie bounced around the kitchen in her cabin singing along to the music blaring out from the TV. She had an incredible night's sleep, and the dream had only added to her good mood. The kiss still lingered on her lips from when Dash had left her at her doorway, and since she had dreamed of him naked and about to make love to her, she had been turned on and bouncing ever since.

She supped hot coffee while flipping pancakes and nodded her head to the beat. She was still in her nightdress and robe, bare footed and bleary eyed, but she was having the time of her life. If every morning in Bridge Hollow could be like this, then she would be a very happy girl indeed.

She sat at the kitchen island and poked at the fresh pancakes with her fork. It really had been an incredible start to her stay in town, but she was starting to feel guilty at the lack of work she had done. Sure, she still didn't have her workstation properly set up and she was still waiting on a desk, but she at least could have turned on her laptop and tried to make sense of some of her ideas. It's not like she couldn't sit on the couch and bash away at the keys for a few hours.

When she finished breakfast, she went back to her bedroom and picked out an outfit for the day. She settled on a long sleeved, black maxi dress and a pair of ankle boots. She showered and did her hair, spritzed on some perfume and dabbed on a little tinted moisturizer and lip stain, before she quickly made her bed, threw open the window and let the fresh mountain air come seeping in to blow away the cobwebs.

She breathed in deep.

It really was so clean and healthy out there. It was nothing like her own town back on the West Coast. She may have had a beach not far away, but she still had endless amounts of traffic and industry to contend with, and there really was nothing like the freshness of the mountains.

When she was back in the living area, she climbed up the ladder to the mezzanine level and looked across to the space where the desk would be. She got down on her hands and knees and cleared stuff away on part of the floor, ensuring everything was where it should be so that, if Dash showed up, she could get the desk in there without a problem.

When she had finished sorting and tidying, she carried up the rest of her work and research and laid it on the floor next to the empty space. Then she looked around and sighed.

She wanted to get going… and she also wanted to see Dash again.

She bit her bottom lip and grinned, before she carefully climbed down the ladder, taking her time so she didn't trip on her own boots. When she reached the kitchen island, she grabbed the piece of paper that had been sitting there since her first night in town, and she tapped it into her cellphone and saved it.

"Should I call or text him?" she wondered out loud as she stared at the screen of her phone.

She knew, if the roles were reversed and he was getting in touch with her, that she would prefer to get a phone call... but for that reason, she decided she would do the opposite and send him a message instead.

"Don't want to be over the top too soon...," she said as she opened the message app and began to type her opening bit.

J: How is a writer supposed to write without a desk? I'm starting to think you forgot about me 😔

She hit send and then threw the phone across the island as if it were on fire. She closed her eyes and cringed. She had never been very good at being the one to text first, and now she was worried she would never get a reply.

Luckily, she didn't have long to wait to be put out of her misery because, within about half a minute, her cellphone sounded with a beep.

D: Forget about you? Come on! I was actually just about to call you... your desk is ready. Are you home?

She grinned from ear to ear and hastily typed her reply.

J: I sure am, come on over x

. . .

She smiled and laid the phone down on the island, and then she found herself pacing the floors of the cabin. The whole place was spotless, and she didn't have anything to do... all she could do was think about Dash and the fact that she was about to see him again any minute.

When he knocked at the door, her heart did a little dance in her chest, and the butterflies in her belly grew stronger and stronger.

She flicked her hair over her shoulders and walked slowly to the front door, her boots clicking against the wood floor.

She could see part of his face through the viewing window at the top of the door, and she could already see how handsome and unshaven he was from a few feet away. It looked like he hadn't shaved that morning and it made her pussy twinge. He looked even sexier with some roughed up stubble, and she thought of what it would feel like to kiss his lips and feel his chin graze against hers.

She opened the door and he stood there looking down on her with his dark eyes. His arms were big and muscular, peeking out of his t-shirt, as his low-slung jeans gave her a glimpse of his taught abs and a small patch of dark hair running down from his navel.

It was exactly like her dream, and she gulped down her nerves.

"Hey!" He smiled with glistening eyes as he leaned forward and planted a perfect, solitary kiss on her lips.

She felt the tingling and the fire between them. Every time they connected, their bond grew stronger. Their souls were fusing together, becoming more in tune and aligned with one another, and she was excited to see how much further they could go.

"Hey!" She smiled as she looked into his eyes.

Jet was next to his feet wagging his tail, and she bent

down and gave him a friendly rub on the head and behind the ears.

"He's never far from your side, is he?" she smiled.

"He's my best friend," Dash said as he whistled, and Jet sat down perfectly and pricked his ears back.

Jannie could see the desk in the driveway behind Dash and she grinned when she saw how beautiful it was. It was clearly old and must have been with him for a long time. It was a dark oak, with strong sturdy legs and a stunning feel about it.

"Wow," she whispered. "What a desk!"

"It was my grandmother's, actually," Dash said with a warm fondness. "When she died, I inherited a few of her things, and this was one of the pieces of furniture I always remembered about her the most."

"It's stunning," she said as she reached out and traced her fingertips across the top of it. "And you just had it sitting in your attic gathering dust?"

Dash shrugged.

"We wolves don't have a whole lot of use for antique desks," he winked.

For a moment, she had almost forgotten that Dash wasn't just a man… that he had an animal living inside him too. He had wolf's blood in his veins. Her heart thumped.

"Thank you so much for lending it to me," she said as she stepped back, leaving the doorway clear for him to bring it in. "Want me to grab one end?"

Dash laughed and shook his head.

"You go get me a beer, and I'll do the rest." He winked, and she bit her lip. She loved his playfulness the most. He had been so serious when they had first met, but now that she knew why, it only made her like him even more. He had been trying to put up a wall, the same as she had, but in the end, they had both been unable to resist the pull.

There was clearly something important and deep between them. Something she had never felt, and now, she knew that he had never felt it either.

She opened the refrigerator and pulled out a bottle of beer, then popped off the cap with the end of a corkscrew. She watched as Dash picked the desk up effortlessly and held it in front of him and over his head as if it were weightless. Shifter strength. The cabin may have been small, but its hall-ways were wide, and the rooms were high. As he made his way through, he looked like a contestant on one of those *world's strongest man* shows, walking with a huge desk above his head like it was a feather.

When he placed it down at the foot of the step ladder that went up to the mezzanine, he turned to look at her and she smiled coyly. Every time their eyes met, she felt something new. Something even deeper and more exciting, and she was beginning to get addicted to the feeling.

Dash was turning into her drug.

She held out the bottle of beer, and he stepped over and took it from her, holding it to his lips and taking a swig.

"Thanks," he said with a gasp after he swallowed. "I needed that."

"Well, you know what they say," she teased. "It's always five o'clock somewhere..."

Dash threw his head back and laughed.

"When you hang with us mountain men, you learn there's no such thing as time," he winked. "We make our own rules."

He looked so handsome standing there, and it was taking all her willpower not to jump on him and pull him down onto the couch. She smiled shyly and hoped she wasn't blushing.

He took a step closer to her and leaned in next to the island.

"I thought about you all last night," he said. "I was worried about you over here…"

"You don't need to worry," she said as she looked into his eyes. "I'm fine… I'm used to taking care of myself, you know…"

"I bet you are," he smirked. "But here, it is different. I just hope that's sinking in and you're listening to what I'm saying."

She nodded and smiled weakly.

"I just wish you could tell me everything," she said.

Dash breathed in and then sighed. His eyes traveled out to the lake and to his cabin on the other side.

"I know I can be here in a split second if I need to be," he said. "But I just want you to be careful, that's all."

It felt so good to have someone caring about her. When she had been with Dylan, he wouldn't have given a shit if she had gone missing for two days, as long as he had gotten her back in the end and then made her pay for it. He had never cared about her safety, only that she was doing what he wanted her to do at all times. Even if that meant sitting in a parked car in a dodgy part of town, completely oblivious, while he went and bought drugs around the corner.

He really was a total low life.

And now that she had met Dash, she couldn't believe she had ever put up with it. She was starting to see the real side of love. The side she hadn't known existed. He wanted what was best for her, and he wanted to protect her.

It was a wonderful feeling.

"So, how do you plan on getting that up there?" she asked as she looked up to the mezzanine level.

Dash took another long drink of his beer and then grinned.

"I'll pull it up," he said matter-of-factly, and then he turned and collected a long, thick twist of rope from by the front door. He came back and smiled and waved it in between them before he went over to the desk and tied the rope around the very center of it with a big knot.

Jannie stood back and watched him as he pulled himself up the step ladder in only two strides and jumped up onto the floor above. She could imagine him being good at rock climbing. His shoulders were so broad, and his arms were so strong, it was as if he were a god. When he looked over the mezzanine level with the other end of the rope in his hands, he used the bannister of the balcony to pull the rope across smoothly and the desk bounced up, with ease, in the air. It brushed against the wall a couple times, making dents in the paint and Jannie had to cover her eyes.

"Don't be such a wuss," Dash teased. "I could repaint that wall in about half an hour."

"Well, I'm holding you to that then," she called back to him. "I don't want to lose my deposit."

Dash winked at her and grinned.

When the desk reached him, he used his spare hand to guide it over the rail and then took hold of it properly and set it down.

"There you go," he said as he slapped his hands together. "Piece of cake."

Jannie clapped her hands appreciatively and made her way up the step ladder.

When she got to the top and stepped into the open space, she couldn't believe how good it looked in there. Dash waited for her to show him exactly where she wanted the desk to go, and once it was in place, she wrapped her arm around him and nestled her head onto the side of his arm.

"Thank you so much," she breathed. "This is such a big help."

"It was nothing," Dash smiled.

He wrapped his arm around her shoulder and then

turned her so that they were looking deep into each other's eyes again. She could see the shining glint of green and the way his pupils widened when he was locked in on her.

She had never been this attracted to someone before. And having him there with her but not tearing his clothes off was absolute torture.

She smiled and he brushed her hair behind her ear and held onto her neck. His hands were so big, and she felt tiny next to him, but she also felt as if they fit together perfectly. There was something so completely arousing about him, and also, something that she adored. It was a pure and warming kind of love. It was like coming home.

Dash moved closer and kissed her on the lips. This time, he didn't hold back, and his tongue searched her mouth, kissing her harder and deeper by the second, and Jannie felt herself melt in his arms. Her whole body was tingling; she gasped as he lifted her up and she wrapped her legs around him. He walked with her to the edge of the desk and sat her down on it, and then he broke their lips apart and looked down at her.

She bit her lip and gripped the waist band of his jeans. She so desperately wanted to undo the buttons and reach inside, but she had to hold back. The feeling of waiting was turning her on even more.

"You really are something else," he said to her with a mischievous smile. "You just turned up and flipped my world on its head."

She grinned back at him and leaned up to kiss him again.

He was right. They really had turned each other's worlds upside down… and they were only just getting started.

For Jannie and Dash, this was the beginning of something life-changing.

CHAPTER 13

To not rip his clothes off had taken all the willpower in the world. They had kissed and moaned, and Jannie knew that things could easily get out of hand, but she managed to put the brakes on before she let Dash claim her.

She wanted him so badly, but she had so much still to think about. To be taken by a shifter wolf wasn't a decision to make lightly. She had to be one hundred percent sure that he wasn't going to break her heart. And she had to be sure that she was up to the challenge.

When Dash and Jet had left her, he had leaned in and kissed her again and his lips had been hot as fire.

"I want to take you out properly," he said. "Tomorrow night?"

Jannie bit her lip and grinned.

"That would be great," she said.

Dash smiled and nodded, and he gave her a wink before he backed slowly out the door and watched her as he moved away.

"I'll call you in the morning," he said.

She watched as he turned away and Jet skipped along next to him. As Dash was about to move out of sight, he looked back over his shoulder and gave her a wave, and she raised her hand and did the same.

She must have been the strongest person in the world to be able to resist him. And he had been good too… she had no idea how he had managed to hold himself back. It so easily could have gotten hot and heavy.

As the night rolled in, Jannie went up to her new office area and sat at the desk. She turned on her laptop and spread her notes out around it, so she could see all the information she had collected.

Once the laptop had powered up, she opened a search engine and typed SHIFTER WOLF. As the results started to appear on the screen, her heart fluttered wildly in her chest and she found her hand shaking as she clicked on some of the links.

Her eyes scanned images of larger than life wolves roaming around forests and mountains. She saw snarling animals, and read stories from people who believed they had seen this particular phenomenon for real.

She had yet to see Dash turn… but she knew it was in there. She had heard and felt the wolf. She knew it was lurking beneath the surface and at the right moment, he would come leaping forward.

She closed the computer and sat back in her chair. She found herself nervously biting the tip of her thumb and she closed her eyes.

This is so unlike you, she thought. *Are you just getting carried away?*

She hated to think that may be the case, because what she felt with Dash was mind-blowing… and yet, she still had her reservations. She didn't like the way he wasn't being one hundred percent open with her about what was happening in Bridge Hollow.

She found herself grumpily getting up from the desk and climbing back down to the main floor, where she lit some scented candles, turned on the television, and found a big tub of ice cream in the bottom freezer drawer.

She was going to have to occupy herself for a while and try not to let her mind be always just on Dash. He was already in her head so much, and she knew that if she wanted to continue seeing him, it was only going to get stronger as their connection grew. And then there was the claiming… if she slept with him… she would be his forever.

Her pussy throbbed.

She liked the idea of being claimed. It turned her on.

"Come on, Jannie," she scolded herself. "You're not doing a very good job of not thinking about him!"

She stomped over to the couch and sat down with the ice cream and dug into it with a spoon. She watched reruns of old sitcoms, ate her treats, and sat by candlelight until it was nearly midnight. When she turned off the TV and blew out the candles, she looked out over the lake and saw that the lights in Dash's cabin were still on and she wondered if he was looking across at her too.

It was so hard to keep walking away from him. She didn't know how much longer she was going to be able to do it.

She closed her eyes and listened to the lapping of the water as the lake softly hit the shore, and then she was sure, in the distance, she heard the howls of wolves.

She smiled.

She was beginning to like that sound.

And she was beginning to like it so much in Bridge Hollow that she was wondering if she would ever want to leave.

. . .

Jannie wandered around town with a big smile on her face as she nursed a take-out coffee in one hand and held her cellphone in the other. Dash had been messaging her all day, and their flirtatious banter was beginning to become the norm. She had never met someone who just seemed to get her, and it truly was as if they had known each other for years.

She dipped in and out of stores on Main Street, looking for inspiration for something to wear that evening. She had no idea where on Earth he was taking her, but she was excited to see, and she wanted to make an effort.

She looked in the windows of the few clothing stores that were dotted around town, and she even found herself browsing through books at a secondhand shop, even though she already had plenty to read. By the time she had been up and down Main Street on one whole side and began down the other, her feet were already beginning to ache and she wondered if she would be better off heading home rather than wearing herself out when she would likely need all her energy for later.

She grinned to herself at the thought.

Even though she was telling herself straight up that she had to be good… her bad side was still wanting to shine. She knew the devil on her shoulder would be telling her to go for it… because the devil knew what she really wanted.

Just as she was about to call it a day, her eye was caught by something purple, and she found herself being drawn toward it. It was the sign out front of one of the stores, and as she got closer, she saw the multicolored beaded curtains in the window, the crystal balls and tarot cards, and the incense burning lightly by the doorway. There was a sign for palm readings, and she stepped a little closer.

This shop looked awesome. She had seen places like this before, but not one in such a small town. She loved the way the whole of Bridge Hollow embraced the legends that surrounded it, and they clearly were into their paranormal subjects.

She looked through the window and wished she had the nerve to go inside. She turned and stared at the palm reading sign again, and then she shrugged her shoulders and thought, *what the hell!*

Inside, the shop was dark, and the scent of incense hung heavily in the air. It was silent, apart from the sound of the wind lightly whistling in through the doorway and the ting of the windchimes that were hanging for sale along one wall. As she walked in further, she looked at the crystals lining the displays, some were big and some were small, but each of them were unique and enchanting.

She stopped and started to flick through the small library section, but it wasn't long before she was aware of someone else in the store with her, and she turned to see an older woman standing there with long silver hair and a kind smile.

"Hello," she said as she took a step toward Jannie.

"Oh, hi," Jannie smiled. "Is this your store?"

The lady nodded. Jannie was trying to figure out how old she was… She was certainly in her late forties at least, but her hair was so silvery white she could have easily been much older. It was her fresh skin and sparkling white eyes which gave her youth away, and Jannie thought she was incredibly beautiful.

"I haven't seen you before," the lady said. "Are you a tourist?"

"Kind of," Jannie admitted with a blush. "I've leased a cabin by one of the lakes, and I'm here to write a book."

"How wonderful," the lady smiled.

She reached down to one of the displays and picked up a blue stone hanging from a silver chain.

"Here," she smiled warmly. "This will help you with your

creativity. Wear it while you work and leave it on your windowsill at night under the light of the moon t0 charge it."

Jannie felt a tingle of excitement as she picked it up and held it in her hands. The longer the stone stayed in her palm, the more she felt the heat of it rising.

"Wow," she said. "Does that really work?"

The lady smiled warmly.

"If you believe, it does," she said as she turned and began to walk to the back of the shop. "Are you a believer?"

Jannie found herself following her and she stopped and started to flick through some of the artwork on one of the stands.

"I always thought so, yes," she said. "I mean, it's pretty hard not to believe here...," she said, trailing off. "This place has a magic all its own."

The lady smiled.

"You're very wise," she said. "And it is lovely to meet you."

The woman held out her hand and Jannie reached out and shook it.

"I'm Beau," she said. "And you are?"

"Jannie," she smiled. "And yes, it's good to meet you too."

Beau let Jannie's hand fall, and then she reached behind her to the counter and picked up a set of tarot cards.

"Do you ever have readings?" she asked her.

Jannie shook her head. She loved the idea of someone being able to tell her fortune and give her guidance, but when it came down to it, she had never truly had the nerve to do something like that.

Beau smiled and rested the cards down.

"I sense you're not as much of a believer as you think," she said wisely.

"No...," Jannie tried to defend herself. "I am... I'm just a little bit scared, that's all."

"And what is there to be scared of?" Beau asked her.

Jannie thought for a moment and shrugged. Since she had come to Bridge Hollow, she had pretty much thrown all her own rules out the window. She had done things and thought things she never would have dared before. She knew and felt deep within that she was on a personal journey of self-growth, and she was loving every second.

"I won't charge you for this," Beau said as she stepped forward and took hold of Jannie's right hand.

Jannie faltered for a moment, but then she relaxed and let Beau look down at her palm for a few moments before her eyes traveled back up to meet hers.

"Someone here has marked you," she said lowly. "Someone important in this town must think a great deal about you…"

She waited for a moment, and Jannie's heartbeat began to rage.

"This man, he loves you…" She stopped and smiled. "But you are both afraid…"

A chill rolled up Jannie's spine.

"The universe has a way of bringing people together, Jannie," Beau continued. "It is much bigger than all of us and we shouldn't fight it."

She let go of her hand but Jannie could still feel the sensation of heat on her palm. In the other hand, the blue crystal throbbed, and she squeezed it tight.

"He's not as terrifying as you think," Beau said. "They have good hearts. They are stronger and kinder than you will ever know."

The two women looked at each other for a moment and Jannie felt something inside her click.

Beau was right.

And it was clear that she had powers all her own.

She nodded in agreement and then she reached into her handbag to get out her wallet.

"Thank you," Jannie smiled. "I mean it. I appreciate you telling me that."

"Listen to your heart," Beau said.

The silence rose between them and Jannie knew that she was right. Beau was a wise woman, and Jannie was glad she had wandered into this delightful little store.

She opened her wallet and went to find some cash to pay for the crystal necklace, but Beau held up her hand to say no.

"You need it," she smiled. "I won't take your money; just promise me you'll use it."

Jannie looked at her for a moment to be sure, but Beau urged her away from the cash desk.

"This town is a good place for you," she said sincerely. "You may be new here, but it is already awakening things in you that will serve you well in your life. If I were you, I would think about your future and what you want from your career and relationships. Think about what you have back where you came from and what you want to keep."

Jannie shook Beau's hand again and thanked her. She felt so much clarity, as if a fog had just been cleared and she could finally see ahead.

As she walked away from the little purple shop and made her way back out onto Main Street and toward the winding country roads that led back to the cabin, Jannie realized that she didn't have a whole lot to go back to her hometown for.

She had friends and she had family, but they all had their own lives, and she had been just kind of waiting around on the edges of all of them. Here, in Bridge Hollow, she was actually living for her. She was the lead in this journey, not her best friend or her cousin. She had a career and a goal, had met a man and was making friends, and she felt connected to something.

She turned the corner and began to walk back down to the cabin. When she saw the front door, she smiled and walked straight around the back to the veranda which looked out over the lake.

She had found a really lovely place in the world. And she wasn't going to be ready to leave in six weeks. Without wasting a second longer, she grabbed her cellphone and started to write an email to the man she had leased the cabin from, requesting to have it for two extra weeks. If, after that time, she was still feeling the same, she may even stay longer and finish the whole book.

Suddenly, her sabbatical was turning into a whole new life.

But she wasn't afraid.

CHAPTER 14

Jannie stood in the kitchen, by the island, sipping a glass of ice-cold white wine while she spun her cellphone around in front of her with her index finger. She hated to admit it, but she had already been ready for half an hour, and she was doing all she could not to pace the floors while she was waiting for Dash.

He had told her he would pick her up at eight, and it was getting closer. She looked up and saw the second hand ticking around and around the clock on the wall. And she willed it to move faster.

She took another sip and looked down at her phone again, but the screen remained blank.

On the other side of the lake, she could see that Jet was lounging on the veranda overlooking the water, and she huffed at knowing Dash must still be at home.

She poured herself a little more to drink and sipped slowly, and when she turned back to look, around five minutes later, she instantly saw that Jet had disappeared and the house looked dark.

The sun had bobbed down behind the mountain, and even though there was still some low light in the air, mostly, the world around them was dark and lit only by the lights dotted around the lake and in the houses.

Jannie bit her bottom lip and tried not to grin. And just when she was about to move to go check her reflection in the mirror one more time, she suddenly heard the roar of an engine.

It made her jump and she clutched her hand to her chest. The engine was revving and getting louder and louder.

"Is that a bike?" she whispered to herself as she started to move slowly to the front door.

When she reached it and looked through the little window, she couldn't help but smile, because this had been the last thing she had been expecting.

Dash was sitting outside, waiting for her on a glinting silver motorcycle, and he was looking sexier than ever. His jeans were black and skinny with rips in the knees, his white t-shirt was skin hugging and showed off his powerful muscles, and the leather jacket he had around his shoulders made him look an absolute Rockstar dream.

Was there anything this guy couldn't do?

He was handsome, intelligent, bad and dangerous, had magical powers... and now, he was turning up to collect her on a Harley!?

She shook her head and laughed as she opened the door and crossed her arms over her chest.

"What the hell is this?" she asked playfully.

"This is my bike," he said as he looked down at her. "Come and get on, baby..."

She grinned and reached back inside to grab her jacket and purse before she locked the door and trotted over to meet him.

Dash kissed her and pulled her close to him. He tasted of whiskey and cigarettes, but he was still completely in control.

"Have you been drinking?" she asked him with a raised brow, looking down at the motorcycle as well and frowning.

"Shifter rules," he winked. "We don't absorb alcohol like you humans do... it barely even touches the sides."

"Lucky," she smiled as she held onto his shoulder and climbed on behind him. He rested his hand on her thigh and gave her a squeeze before he revved the engine again and pulled her arms around his waist.

"Where are you taking me, anyway?" she asked as she rested her head on his shoulder so that her mouth was close to his ear.

"For a ride... and then for a drink," he said. "I think we need to blow off some steam, don't you?"

Jannie gripped him a little tighter and nodded her head. He sure was right about that, and she couldn't think of anything she would rather do than disappear on the open road with him.

He revved the engine and kicked up a spray of gravel as he floored the bike and they seemed to fly up the slope and toward the main mountain roads.

Jannie had never been on the back of a motorcycle before, so it was another first to add to her ever-growing list of things that had happened to her since she had come to Bridge Hollow. Beau had been right when she said this place was good for her; it was as if she were finally letting herself go and starting to live.

As Dash swerved the bike around the mountain roads, Jannie gripped him tightly but made sure she held her head back so she could see it all. It felt like she was flying; the wind whipped her skin and blew her hair around her eyes and into her mouth, but she didn't mind, she was having the time of her life.

Dash slowed as they took the main stretch in to Bridge Hollow and flew out the other side of town. Jannie had come in from the other direction and had no idea where they were headed, but she was happy to leave it in his hands.

He decelerated as they reached a bend, and as they approached the edge of the road, she could see that a huge valley was laid out before them. Mountains flanked either side, and straight down the middle, the sun was setting. One of the mountains must have hid the sun from her vantage point at the lake, but there, she could see it about to disappear at its lowest point, and it was a stunning sight to see.

Dash stopped the bike with a crunch after it hissed along the gravel and then he turned to her and smiled.

"How was that?" he asked her with a grin.

"Exhilarating," she laughed. "Seriously, I think I'm shaking."

Dash stepped off the bike and held out his hand for Jannie to take hold. When she did, he helped her climb off and he stood behind her, wrapping his arms around her waist.

"I wanted you to see this view," he said. "You only get it at this time of the year, and only for a few weeks… and it just so happens, it's right about now."

The autumn sun was low, and it was turning the valley ahead of them orange and gold. It reflected off the water of some of the lakes and turned them into liquid sunshine.

"It's beautiful," she whispered.

The air seemed cleaner and crisper, and she felt a deep connection to where she was standing. Dash's arms were heavy and protective around her, and they made her feel so very safe, even with all the danger that was unfolding not far away.

"I love it here," she said.

"It's a pretty great view," he confirmed.

"Not just out here tonight, though," she said. "I mean, Bridge Hollow in general. I don't think I ever want to leave."

Dash kissed the side of her neck and breathed her in.

"Well, maybe you should stay then..." He said it as he kissed her ear, and she felt a tingling sensation run right through her.

Her knees were like jelly and her pussy was aching for him. She didn't know how much longer she was going to be able to resist him, and she wished, in that split second, that they were back at her cabin, not out in the wilderness without a bed to fall into.

"You drive me wild," she whispered as she turned around and stared up into his eyes.

He kept his arms wrapped tightly around her and squeezed the base of her back.

"You have no idea what you're doing to me," he said, and his voice seemed deeper and gruffer. The green tinge came back to his eyes and his pupils grew wide.

He leaned in and kissed her, and she melted into him. The sensation of his kiss was deep and powerful, and she lost herself in the moment, never wanting it to end.

When their lips separated, and she saw how green and bright his eyes had become, she smiled and looked down shyly. She was becoming less and less afraid of what may happen if she made a further step with this dangerous man... because she could tell he was completely worth it.

"Come on," he growled as he grinned and pulled her closer to him. "Let's get out of here and go somewhere we can have some fun. I need a drink or I'm going to ravage you right here and now."

He slapped her ass and she squeaked with laughter before he picked her up at the waist and placed her on the back of the bike. When he climbed on ahead of her, she wrapped her arms straight around him and pulled herself into him. She pressed her pussy right up against him and squeezed her legs tight. She was so turned on and wished she could be with him right there and then, but he was right. They had a whole night ahead of them, and he had promised to take her out. She wanted to go somewhere fun with him and drink some beers before, hopefully, getting to know him even more.

He revved the engine and started to ride.

Being on the back of a Harley with Dash was already turning into her new favorite thing.

THE BAR WAS ON THE HIGHWAY, FULL OF TRUCKERS AND tourists, but a hotspot for fun and debauchery. When Dash pulled into the parking lot and stopped the bike, he looked over his shoulder to gauge her reaction.

"What do you think?" he asked.

"It's different," she laughed. "But I get it… we won't see anyone we know out here, and we can have a proper conversation?"

"Bingo," he grinned. "Being here means I get you all to myself and no one will interrupt us."

He jumped off the side of the bike and helped Jannie down.

"I used to come here when I was a kid," he laughed. "Everyone in town knew me and knew that I was underage, so when I hit eighteen, my friends and I used to drive out here with fake IDs."

"Terrible," Jannie teased. "What was the point, when alcohol doesn't even affect you?"

"Just a rite of passage, I guess," he smiled. "It's not as if I grew up like most of the regular folk in Bridge Hollow…"

Jannie felt sorry for him for a second; she couldn't even imagine what it must be like for someone like him having to keep such a massive secret.

"Do most people in town not know?" she asked.

Dash shook his head.

"The regular folk in town don't have a clue. It's always been the norm for them to have these rumors and they think everyone plays up to it, if they do have an inkling, then they definitely turn a blind eye. No one wants any trouble and it brings a lot of tourism and money to the town. Without the legends, who knows where we would all be."

"It must be frightening then… all these strange happenings…?" Jannie didn't want to probe too much, but at the same time, she felt like she did want an explanation. Especially, when she was going to be staying there for even longer. She didn't like having information withheld from her.

"Yeah," Dash said. And she sensed a wall had instantly come up. "Yeah, it is."

He gripped her hand and started to walk toward the door of the bar, and she knew then that the conversation was over. He was back to being cagey, and she was starting to feel uneasy. She didn't want to ruin the evening, but at the same time, she wanted him to open up to her.

As they walked inside, the music hit them. The bar, compared to the places in Bridge Hollow, was completely wild; there were bikers and scantily clad women everywhere.

"Wow," she laughed. "Now I see why you liked coming here when you were eighteen."

Dash laughed and wrapped his arm around her as he led her to the bar and then kissed her on the shoulder. Every time his lips connected with her skin, she felt a pulse of heat and a rush of excitement. Their bond was so strong already and, with each touch, their souls were becoming more entwined.

The bartender made his way to them, and Dash ordered a beer and a whiskey chaser.

Jannie thought on what she wanted for a moment, and then she decided she would have another glass of wine.

"I can't promise it'll be nice in here," Dash laughed. "I mean, look at this place."

"I'll give it a whirl," she smirked. "How bad can it really be?"

When she tasted it, her eyes began to water, and Dash threw his head back and howled with laughter.

"Your face," he said. "I wish you could have seen that."

"Jeez," she grimaced. "You were right, I should have listened to you."

"Come on then, what would you like instead?" He grinned and leaned back into the bar.

"Vodka, on the rocks," she winked.

She was going to try out her new bad girl persona and see if she liked it.

Dash winked and called to the bartender over as Jannie turned to watch the crowd.

They were so drunk and all over the place. Men and women grinding up against each other, girls wearing ripped fishnets and the truckers grinning as they drank their beers. The whole place oozed sex, and she wondered how many other places there were like this around town.

"Here." Dash handed her the glass.

"This place is giving me the creeps," she half laughed. "These women look like they're just here to hook up."

"They probably are," said Dash. "It's a truck stop."

"Why don't we just go back to my place?" she asked with a raised brow. "You can teach me how to light the stove… and I have wine."

Dash smiled at her and then he wrapped an arm around her and kissed her on the side of the head.

"I agree, this place has gone slightly downhill," he cringed. "I wasn't expecting this."

"It's okay," she laughed. "But seriously, come on, let's get the hell out of here."

Dash began to walk with her to the exit, and when they reached the door and headed out into the clear and wonderful night, her uneasiness had subsided. Jannie had never felt happier.

CHAPTER 15

*D*ash closed the front door behind him as Jannie kicked off her boots and padded along the wood floor of the hallway to the kitchen and living area.

It was pitch black inside the cabin, and there was a definite chill in the air, something deeper and more wintery than there had been any other night she had been there.

She stopped at the island and placed her purse and jacket down before she wrapped her arms around herself.

"It's so cold," she whispered.

Dash walked in slowly and started to sniff the air. She saw the glint in his green eyes and saw them getting brighter.

He paused and then he looked over to her.

"Is it like this in here every night?" he asked.

She shook her head.

"And you said there was a stove?" He looked around and his eyes settled on it. "Okay," he smiled. "Let's get it lit."

He was acting completely normal, but Jannie had the feeling there was something else going on with him, as if he were cautious of something. The cold really was intense. She shivered and opened the cupboard to pull out two big wine glasses and a bottle of smooth red.

Dash got down on his knees in front of the stove, and even though it was pitch black, he began to get to work. Jannie felt a rush of excitement as she realized his vision must be powerful. She poured them both a glass and began to walk around the room, lighting candles and lanterns as she came to them, and casting wonderful shadows around the cabin walls. When she was done, she took both glasses and the bottle over to the couch and sat down to watch him.

She had never lit a fire before. Not even when she had been camping as a kid, and she watched as Dash worked quickly with his hands, placing the logs together inside the stove so they were arranged almost like a teepee.

The fire caught quickly, and he closed the door to the stove and opened a vent at the bottom which made the air rush in and the flames roar up the flume.

"Thank you," she smiled. "This feels amazing."

He turned and looked at her and smiled back.

He walked over to her and sat down on the couch, and Jannie leaned in to him and passed him his glass. He wrapped his arm around her, and they sat there sipping their wine and enjoying each other's company.

"Tell me," she said finally. "Why did you take me to that weird bar tonight?"

Dash stiffened, as if he knew he had been caught out, and he hung his head and let out a little laugh.

"Do you know everything?" he smiled.

"I feel like I know you," she said genuinely. "And I feel like I can tell when you're not being one hundred percent honest."

He nodded his head slowly and then sighed and turned to her.

"The only reason I'm not telling you what you want to

know is because I'm trying to protect you," he said. "I want you to try and put yourself in my shoes… Imagine meeting the one person in the world you had been waiting your whole life for, but then, at the same time, everything you had ever known was at risk. There were forces around you that you didn't fully understand, and you were afraid to drag this person into it."

She smiled weakly at him and lowered her head. She was trying to understand, but because she was so in the dark, it was hard.

"I don't want anything to happen to you," he said genuinely. "I don't even know what I'm truly up against, but this chill in the air tonight, and all the strange happenings… I know it's all connected. And I'm worried. I took you to the bar on the highway, so we were well out of the way. I don't know, I just had a bad feeling… as if something terrible might happen."

Jannie's blood ran cold and she gripped his hand.

"I don't trust Bridge Hollow right now," he said. "I can sense something bad has found its way here… and until I've found it, I'm going to be on my guard."

"But surely, out here at the lake we're safe?" she asked. "I haven't seen anything since I've been here, and tonight is the first time I have felt the cold this way."

Dash shook his head.

"We're starting to wonder how far this thing reaches," he said. "But I can't say anymore, I've already said too much, please…"

He trailed off and rubbed his temples, and Jannie sat forward and put her hands on his knees.

"I'm sorry," she said. "I won't probe anymore."

She smiled at him and their eyes locked in on each other's. Dash was clearly conflicted. It was obvious to Jannie that he had a lot going on, but he didn't want to lose her and miss out on their connection, so he was still trying to have some kind of normal life. But she was starting to wonder at what cost.

"Top up?" she asked as she leaned forward and got the bottle.

"Here," he smiled. "Let me."

He took the bottle from her gently and filled her glass first before he moved to his own. When he rested it back down on the coffee table, he turned to her and held his glass in between them.

"A toast," he said as Jannie raised her glass to meet his. "To all that is good in this world, and for all we have yet to learn."

He chinked his glass against hers and Jannie smiled and sipped.

They cuddled together on the couch until the fire in the stove had almost burned away. They finished the wine together and talked about their hopes and dreams. Even when there was a silence between them, it didn't feel bad. There was no pressure to fill it, it was clear they were content in each other's company.

When the clock on the wall said it was getting close to 2am, Jannie felt her eyes dropping and she cuddled into him and relaxed even more. She easily could have stayed there forever, resting on him by candlelight in that perfect little cabin.

She wasn't aware of herself drifting off to sleep, and when she woke again, she was in her bed, tucked up tight and morning had already rolled around.

She sat up with confusion and looked around the room. She was still fully clothed from the night before, but some-how, she was in her bed. She stood and walked to the living area and saw that the candles had been snuffed out, and the fire had turned to ash in the grate of the stove. She saw the two used glasses and the empty bottle of wine had been placed neatly on the counter, so she knew she wasn't imagining it all. Dash had been there with her.

Suddenly, her eyes caught sight of something on the island, and she smiled as she realized it was a piece of paper, the same piece of paper he had written his number on that first night back in Shifter's Bliss. But, this time, he had turned it over and scrawled a note to her on the back…

GOOD MORNING! I HAD TO GET JET AND TAKE HIM OUT. HE *destroys the house if he's left too long, and I didn't want to wake you. You sleep like a baby. Will call you when I get home later. D x*

A WARM, FUZZY FEELING FILLED HER INSIDES AND SHE HELD the paper to her chest and smiled.

This man was totally changing everything for her.

She was falling in deep.

CHAPTER 16

After a full day of writing and exploring her creative side, Jannie sat back in her chair and surveyed the number of pages she had done. The counter in the corner of the document on her laptop read thirty-five, and she grinned from ear to ear.

She had never had a writing day like it, she really had blasted through the opening of her book, and she was all kinds of excited.

As she read over what she had written, she looked down at her cellphone and was disappointed that she still didn't have a message or call from Dash. She felt herself pouting and she crossed her arms over her chest and sighed.

She climbed down the ladder from the mezzanine and into the living area, where she started to potter around, clearing away cups and plates that she had left out from lunch. She spritzed the counters with cleaner and wiped them, making them shine and the whole room smell amazing.

After she had washed and dried the dishes, she was about to go to her bedroom and get changed when she felt her cellphone vibrate in her pocket. She smiled as she reached in and pulled it free, and when she turned it over to look at the screen, she was surprised to see that it was a blocked call trying to come through.

"Hello?" she said as she held it to her ear.

The line was crackling and stayed silent for a moment, then she heard a deep breath and then a familiar voice.

"Hey," Dash said faintly. "It's me."

"Hey," she said brightly as she gripped the phone to her ear and started to walk around the room.

"How's little Jannie?" Dash's voice spoke, but she was sure there was a gravely edge to it, as if he needed to clear his throat.

"I'm good," she smiled. "Missing you, though."

"I miss you too," he said. His voice seemed to crack a little and it made Jannie frown. This wasn't the usual kind of call she would have with Dash. Something sounded wrong.

"Are you okay?" she asked him. "You sound... strange..."

"I need you to come and meet me," he said. "Out in the forest."

Jannie's heart seemed to dip low, right down to her belly, and she coughed slightly and swallowed.

"Okay," she said slowly. "Why? What's going on, are you all right?"

"Just come now," he said quickly. His voice seemed to snap at her, and she jumped back a little on the spot.

"Okay," she whispered. "Are you sure you're all right?"

"I'm halfway up the mountain," he said. "Not far from the abandoned mine. I want to tell you everything."

Jannie's blood shivered right through her and she was already moving toward the door, reaching for her coat and boots as she quickly told him she was on her way.

"Okay, babe," she said. "I'll be there soon."

"Be quick, Jannie," Dash's voice was cold and emotionless. "Be quick."

She ended the call and stopped. It had been such a weird conversation, and he had almost not sounded truly like him. As if he were sick or calling from a million miles away.

She pulled on her coat and buttoned it up to protect her from the horrific cold that had stayed overnight, and as she threw open the door, she slipped her cellphone into her back pocket and locked the door behind her.

She marched straight toward the curve that led up to the main part of the mountain. She hadn't been up these roads before; since she had arrived in town, it had been made clear to her that she should stay well away from there. But now, Dash had called her and said he was ready to tell her everything. He said he was somewhere up there, close to the mine. Now, she just had to stick to the path and find him.

She walked quickly, and it wasn't long before her heart was pounding, and her mouth was dry. She was practically running up a steep slope, trying not to lose her footing as she weaved in and out of rocks and tree roots.

The higher she got, the clearer the air became, but with that also came the cold. She wrapped her arms around herself, and as she got further into the trees, the dark seemed to be heading out toward her, as if it were reaching out, trying to sweep her inside. It was heavy and like a cloak in the sky, and she shivered as she saw her breath catching on the cold air in front of her.

"Dash?" she called out as she stopped on the spot and spun around.

She didn't know where the mine was, but her instincts had led her there, to this point, and she was feeling things she had never even imagined could exist. The cold in the air made the hairs on her head feel chilled to the root. She began to feel dizzy and light as she staggered to the side and clutched the frozen trunk of a pine tree.

"Dash?" she said again. "Where are you?"

Her lip began to wobble, and she was afraid. She had come looking for him, but she had the terrible feeling she was lost and something bad was lurking near her.

She closed her eyes and tried not to succumb to the cold. The darkness was so heavy now that it could easily have been the dead of night, and around her, deep within the forest, she heard the snapping of branches and footsteps running, as if she were being circled by an unknown force.

She opened her eyes and held her hands up to her mouth. She tried to blow on them to get some heat into them, but they seemed to be frozen in place.

She barely dared move and she no longer dared call out for Dash. Her body was shaking, and her brain was freezing, she was dizzy and overcome with dread, and she felt like she didn't know who she was or where she had come to be.

The crunch of frozen ground came from behind her again, and she leaned back against the tree trunk and tried to sink down to the ground, but her legs had been frozen stiff, and she couldn't make them bend. She felt a tear prick the corner of her eye, but it froze in place, and it was then that she knew something awful was most certainly out there in the woods with her.

She held her breath and waited, hoping that whatever it was would move on past her and not realize she was there. But the snapping and crunching of the icy ground got closer and closer, as did the cold, and when it had become too much to bear, she was aware of a dark shadow moving out of the corner of her right eye and she turned and was faced with everything she had been dreading.

He stood there, his face grey and pale, his eyes black and menacing, and from his lips and sharpened teeth, blood dripped slowly onto the icy ground below. He sniffed the air and smiled. This thing. This creature. It looked like a vampire.

Jannie tried not to cry out, and instead, she pushed herself back against the trunk of the tree, hoping he wouldn't see her, but, of course, it was too late.

The vampire stopped in his tracks and his head slowly turned.

When his eyes settled on her, it took only a moment for his grin to split wide, and she saw his terrible jaws fully extend. His teeth were large and sharp, dripping with fresh blood, and the cold was coming from him and from deep within the earth, as if he were a part of whatever had infected the land around her and the rest of Bridge Hollow. He took a step forward and Jannie tried to call out, but as if some kind of spell had been put on her, she found that she was unable to move her mouth, or even her hands. It was as if she had been paralyzed down the full length of her body and there was nowhere to turn.

In her chest, her heart ached. She longed for her protector, and she felt another tear spring free.

What had she done?

"Little Jannie," the vampire creature said with a hiss... and she heard the same voice she had heard on the phone call.

It hadn't been Dash who had asked her to come to these woods high up the mountain. It had been this creature from hell. And now, he had her there, and she was trapped. She couldn't move, the whole world was freezing around her and there was no way out.

"You...," she managed to croak through her frozen lips. "What are you?"

The vampire took another step closer and smiled a wicked smile.

"I'm here to survey," he said. "And get those wolves and

bears out of the way…" He had such delight in his voice. He was nothing but pure evil.

"Why?" she gasped. With each passing second and each intake of breath, she was finding it harder and harder to move, her insides were filling with ice cold air and turning her to stone from within.

"For the rest of us," he smiled.

Jannie clamped her eyes shut and battled against the pain. She shivered on the spot, her whole body aching with the frost, and she felt him as he moved closer and kept her in his sights.

"The head wolf," the vampire spoke. "He will come for you."

Jannie tried to shake her head.

This whole thing was a trap. Dash had made her promise him she would never come up to the mine, no matter what, and she had been stupid. She should have known he would never have asked her to come. How had she been so foolish?

"N…n…no," she gasped, keeping her eyes closed.

Her body felt heavy and she was beginning to get drowsy. She was completely frozen in place and she felt herself being lulled into a dark and deadly slumber.

As the cold gripped her, and her mind began to fade, she was aware of the roars coming from somewhere below on the mountain. She felt the ground shaking beneath her and she forced herself to wake up. The vampire was grinning even wider now, knowing that his plan had worked. He rubbed his hands together and licked his lips, as the noise coming up the mountain got louder and more ferocious.

The air in the forest suddenly got a blast of heat as four gigantic bears and six massive wolves jumped into the clearing, growling and howling.

The vampire spun around on the spot, and Jannie saw his face fall. His wicked grin and sure attitude had all but vanished as he took a step back and bumped up against a pine tree.

The bears began to circle him, and their roars were so loud that they made the ground shake.

The wolves bared their teeth and flanked the bears, readying themselves to attack. It was an incredible sight, and Jannie didn't know if it was real or if she was in a dream.

"No," the vampire said. "This isn't right… You all fight each other."

And that's when it started to click.

The vampire had been counting on the wolves to come up the mountain alone. He hadn't expected the bears to arrive too, and for them to have double the strength and power.

Jannie felt the heat returning to her as the shifters circled the clearing and rounded the vampire into the middle. The wolves snapped and growled their big jaws and with each step closer to the vampire they took, Jannie could see that, even though he knew he was screwed, he was still enjoying the chase.

The bears all reared up on their hind legs and roared so loud the pine trees shook and icicles fell from their branches, smashing to the ground.

"Even if you destroy me," the vampire said, "there are still more… and they will come for you."

Jannie flexed her hands and realized she could move them, and it was then that she managed to pry herself free from her frozen spot on the trunk, and she could see the huge black wolf with the incredible green eyes that was coming toward her.

The cold seemed to grip her again and she seized up. Her vision becoming cloudy.

The wolf brushed up beside her and moved her backward. He moved her away from the raging war in the center of the clearing and the heat coming from his body woke Jannie up and saved her from slipping into unconsciousness. She looked into the wolf's eyes and smiled.

"Dash," she said as she reached up and touched him on the side of the face.

His fur was thick and soft, and his power was overwhelming. When she felt him in wolf form, she felt her heart open, she felt her soul binding with his and she knew then that he had imprinted on her.

He had resisted for so long, and now that he was there, and the extent of his true animalistic nature was shining through, he hadn't been able to go any longer.

And she hadn't wanted him to.

In that moment, they had both wanted it so badly; their hearts had sealed them together as one.

She rested her forehead against his and his heat morphed into her. She closed her eyes and breathed him in, and she wrapped her arms around him as he nudged her back further and further to safety. When she was well away from the clearing, the wolf rubbed up against her. He was so big and frightening, but she wasn't scared of him at all.

She waited and watched as his green eyes glinted and then he turned and ran back to the clearing and into the fight. The vampire was in the center of the circle of wolves and bears, and it was holding its hands up high.

Jannie didn't know what she was bearing witness to, but she could tell it was intense and dark magic. Above the forest, the sky turned black and a flash of silver lightening moved across it, lighting up storm clouds and making them appear ghostly and thick. The wind began to rage and the trees in the clearing were bending with the force.

Jannie kept her gaze fixed on Dash and she prayed for him as she saw him bearing his wolf teeth, growling and howling and snapping his jaws. The vampire was trying to control the wind and the storm raging around them, but she could see that the shifters were all ready to get him and it wouldn't be much longer. The bears closed in on the circle and began to block him from the heavens above, and the wolves snapped and started to nip out at him, tearing at him piece by piece with their ferocious teeth.

The vampire didn't scream; he simply turned and stared at Jannie with a wicked grin and menace in his eyes as the wolves began to tear him apart. If he was experiencing pain, he certainly wasn't showing it, and she saw Dash finally jump up high and crash down on him in the middle of the circle, before all the bears and wolves descended and tore him to shreds, leaving nothing left on the ground but a bloody smudge of black.

Jannie collapsed against the tree and cried out in pain. Her whole body was aching, and she was growing weary again. The cold was still there in the forest and as she saw the shifters begin to turn back into their human form, it was Dash she watched as his fur ripped and gave way to skin as he turned slowly from the large incredible wolf into the man she loved.

She laid on the ground and felt herself slipping out of consciousness. And it wasn't until she felt his strong and protective arms around her, scooping her up from the ground and holding her close to his naked chest, that she felt safe again.

Her protector had come for her and he had saved her.

Her magical wolf.

The love of her life.

She nuzzled into him as she felt herself drift away…

She was safe now, in Dash's arms.

The warmth beneath her relieved her aching bones, and as she rolled onto her side and felt the wrap of warm duvet around her, she smiled and slowly opened her eyes.

Her memory was sketchy, and it took her a few moments to figure out where she was, but when she saw her closet door hanging half open, she smiled and was so relieved to be home in the cabin. She pushed herself up slowly and leaned against the headboard.

What the hell had happened?

She felt as if she had been hit by a truck. It was like she had the worst hangover of her life and a deep chill in her bones. She rubbed her head and pulled her hand away and found a pine needle in her hair… and it was then that it all came rushing back.

The vampire.

The fight.

The woods and the trick.

She had been lured there and had put Dash in danger. But

he had saved her, and he and the wolves had defeated the evil.

She jumped to her feet and tried to steady herself so that she wouldn't fall. She was walking on wobbly legs, as if she were still getting used to her ankles, and she rested against the door frame and looked down the hall toward the living area.

"Hey, sleepy head." Dash's voice came from behind her, and she spun on the spot and gasped.

She felt tears well up in her eyes and she fell into him, wrapping her arms around him, and never being so relieved to have seen anyone so much in her entire life.

She sobbed into his chest and he stroked her head and hair with his hand.

"It's okay," he whispered to soothe her. "I'm here, it's okay."

"I'm so sorry," she sobbed. "It was all my fault."

Dash took hold of her face and cupped it in his hands as he looked her deep in the eyes and shook his head.

"It wasn't your fault," he said sternly. "None of us could have predicted how that would unfold. I'm just so sorry the evil used you to lure us there."

He pulled her into his chest again and wrapped his big arms around her shoulder. Behind him, she could see that the bathroom was steaming up; he had run a hot bath, filled with soap suds.

"You need to get in the tub," he said. "Your body temperature is low; it'll help bring it back up."

She nodded and let him scoop her up in his arms while she wrapped hers around his neck. He carried her to the bathroom, and she stood in front of him as he reached for her clothes and started to peel them from her. When he lifted her top off over her head and she stood there naked in front of him, his breath seemed to catch in his throat. She was so turned on, and even though her bones were still aching, her pussy was throbbing for him.

He peeled away her trousers and underwear and threw them on the floor, and then he lifted her at the waist and placed her in the tub. She sat in the water and let it flow over her, and Dash stood by the side and watched her.

"How does that feel?" he asked, his eyes skimming every inch of her.

"Good," she moaned. "But it would feel even better if you were in here with me…"

She smiled, and Dash's eyes glinted.

She had been waiting for this moment since the second she had laid eyes on him, and now, he had imprinted on her and she had made her choice. She wanted to give herself to him properly. She wanted them to be together forever. She was his love. And she wanted him to claim her.

She held out her hand, and he rose to his feet. She could see he had scratches and cuts where he had been hurt as the wolf, but they were quickly healing before her very eyes and he looked so strong standing there with his bare chest and heaving muscles.

She watched intently as he reached for the buttons on his jeans and popped them open, one by one. When he started to slide them over his hips and his boxers came with them, she held her breath as she waited for his huge and completely perfect cock to spring free.

Her eyes widened, and Dash smirked.

He was so hard and thick. It was the biggest she had ever seen, and she pulled him close to her, urging him to climb into the tub. It was big, much bigger than the one she had back in her hometown, and it was almost as if the person who had installed it had exactly this in mind. Jannie pushed Dash against the side of the tub and she climbed up on his lap, wrapping her legs around him and kissing him hard on the mouth.

Her pussy was so wet and slick for him, and as she eased herself up and onto him, she groaned as he filled her good and proper. Dash grunted and she could still see the wolf behind his eyes. They flickered with the intense green and his pupils were wide and engulfing.

"My God," he groaned as she rose up on him and then slid down the full length of his shaft. She hadn't been able to wait a moment longer, and with each thrust of her hips and every time she lifted and brought herself back down on him, she felt a heat inside her increasing, and him getting harder and harder inside of her.

The water sloshed up around them, and the foam from the suds blew up into the air like bubbles in the wind.

She leaned forward and kissed him, and he gripped her soft, supple breasts with his incredibly strong and masculine hands. When she paused for a moment and let him kiss her neck and up to her ear, she quivered and sensed the power in him surging forward.

"I want to take you hard," he said as he held onto her and got to his feet.

She still had her legs wrapped around him and his cock was still buried deep inside of her, but he walked with her out of the bathroom and to the bed where they collapsed and he kissed her again all down her chest and up her neck.

She was engorged and his cock was so hot and powerful, when he bent her leg and lifted it high, so he could drive himself into her further, Jannie braced herself.

This was it.

Dash grunted and growled, and within him, a ferocious power came to the surface. Behind his eyes, she saw the wolf, and as he fucked her and made her his, she moaned and began riding the most intense waves of pleasure she had ever known.

Dash's strokes became harder and faster, and his huge, bulging shoulders and arms held her down on the bed as he worked up to his release and the moment she had been waiting for.

His cock thrust up inside her and he hit her deep in all the right places, a heat rocketing up her spine and right inside her cunt, making her juices drip for him as his cock thumped and pumped.

When she felt him beginning to tense, she couldn't hold on any longer either. Jannie gripped him tight with her ankles and bit his shoulder as her orgasm surged through her. Her body bucked and shook beneath him, and Dash growled and howled up to the ceiling as he spilled his seed inside of her.

She cried out and collapsed as he flattened out on top of her, and their foreheads touched. She had never felt love like it before, her whole body quivered, and her bones were shaking.

"My god," she panted as she smiled up at him, and he leaned in to kiss her.

The feeling was out of this world. It wasn't sex. It wasn't even making love. This had been much more than that. It was a life-changing experience.

Now, Dash had claimed her, and now, she was his for the rest of time.

They clung together in the messed-up bedsheets and both fell into a deep sleep. The day had been wild and drained them both of their energy. But now that they were fully joined together, it wouldn't take them long to recover.

Two halves had become a whole... and their power was endless.

.   .   .

Jannie woke to Dash kissing her shoulder and holding her tightly from behind. He spooned her, and the warmth she felt between their bodies was soothing and calm. She moaned and pushed her ass back into his crotch and she felt him grip her harder.

"Tease," he said sleepily as he kissed her again and then rolled her over, so they could look into each other's eyes.

His cuts and grazes from the fight had completely disappeared and he held her there in his incredibly powerful arms and traced his fingertips up and down her perfectly soft skin.

"I can't believe I've found you," he said with a smile. "I never imagined how amazing it was going to be."

Jannie smiled back at him and had to agree. This was amazing. It was more than she had ever dreamed. When she had come to Bridge Hollow, with a vague idea of a story in her head about a shifter, she had no idea she would meet one for real. Let alone, fall in love and be claimed by one, a brutally handsome Alpha Wolf who had now saved her life in more ways than she could count.

She reached up and touched his neck, running her hands through the back of his hair.

"I'm staying here now," she said. "I already extended the cabin by two weeks."

"Well," Dash grinned. "You better cancel it."

Jannie furrowed her brow and looked at him sternly.

"Because there's no way I'll be able to stand you being all the way over on this side of the lake," he laughed.

Jannie slapped him playfully on the arm.

"I want you over there with me." His eyes sparkled. "You're my woman… the other half of me… you can't be over here."

She bit her bottom lip and smiled.

"Okay," she said. "I'll sort it out."

Dash pushed his forehead up against hers, and it

reminded her of the wolf inside him. How, when he had saved her, he had done the same thing to calm her and reassure her.

This man was so incredible. He truly had stolen her heart.

"Plus, with everything that's happening," he said, "I'll want you close by."

"But you defeated the vampire..." Jannie said. "Doesn't that mean everything is okay now?"

Dash smiled sadly and shook his head.

"I have a feeling this is only just the beginning..."

Jannie remembered something... a snippet of conversation... cold words spoken with malice. And she saw the vampire's face and the way he had grinned when he had told her he was there to survey Bridge Hollow and make sure the bears and wolves were out of the way... *for the rest of us...*

"There's more of them," she said. And Dash nodded. "He told me, out there in the woods. Before you all got there, he told me he was there to clear the way for the rest of his kind."

Dash exhaled and looked down.

"We had the feeling," he said. "And when we turned up to see his surprise that we had joined together, well, that's when I knew... their energy had been trying to drive us apart and encourage inter-pack wars. Luckily, we solved all our disagreements before he came here. And we had a little extra help from an old friend higher up on the mountain."

Jannie looked at him and cocked her head, but Dash shook his.

"Trust me," he said, "you've had enough to deal with for one day. Let's just enjoy this time together, just me and you... before everything goes crazy again."

"And do you think it will?" she asked. "Go crazy, I mean?"

Dash rubbed his temples.

"I think we're in for a bumpy ride," he said. "But, this time, we know more about what we are up against... and we'll be ready."

Jannie cuddled into him and closed her eyes.

This man was so strong, she didn't know how he did it. He was truly incredible, and she knew how lucky she was to have found him.

"I'm so lucky," he said, as if he had read her mind, "to have you by my side. You're an amazing woman."

Jannie felt the love between them and she reached down as they took hold of each other's hands. Dash lifted hers to his lips and kissed it softly and as they laid together, and the sky outside got darker and darker, Jannie knew she had found her true place in the world.

She had come to Bridge Hollow to research a book, but she had quickly found that the real research she had needed to do was on herself. She had embarked on an intense journey of self-discovery, and had found something life-changing and amazing along the way. In letting down her walls and opening herself up to some of her biggest fears, she had found danger, but she had also found the love of her life and the man who had been looking and waiting for her all along. Maybe all the danger and hard times she had experienced before Bridge Hollow hadn't been to break her... but to build her up and get her ready for the fight to come.

She was prepared for whatever was to come their way. And with Dash by her side, she knew they could take on anything.

ive weeks later…

As October got into full swing, Bridge Hollow enjoyed a lull of activity from deep within the forest. The cold winds and ice stayed at bay, but the threat still remained. Dash looked out across the lake and sniffed the air. He had spent the morning out, running as the wolf, with Jet by his side. And now that he had returned home, he was eager to get moving on the next task at hand. He had to arrange the next recon group of his pack to go out into the forests and mountains, to try to find how the evil had slipped past the dragons at the mine. Somewhere, there was another break… a portal between two worlds that was letting in danger. But he had to remain positive. They had defeated one vampire; maybe this would mean the others wouldn't take so lightly coming here and trying to overtake a power they didn't fully understand.

When shifters bonded together, the whole world took notice.

They were a force of god.

He looked back over his shoulder and saw Jannie in the kitchen. She was busying herself at the island, typing away furiously at her laptop and chewing her bottom lip. Since she had moved in with him and brought the old desk back with her, she had had no end to inspiration. Being immersed in a shifter household was certainly working for her, and she had adapted well. She tapped at the keys and he could see the determination etched on her face. He had read some of her work and had loved seeing how her mind ticked. For the protagonist to be a girl from a small town, moving to the mountains and meeting a shifter wolf, he had to enjoy being the main source of her inspiration, and he looked forward to the day he would see it on the shelves and be able to hold the book in his hands. He had every faith in Jannie, and he knew her dreams would come true when it came to her career. She had a tenacity he found endearing, and he was so proud to have her there with him. He was honored that she had chosen to spend her life with him and let him be a part of all she had to offer the world.

He smiled and watched as Jet wandered slowly into the kitchen on tired legs and brushed up against her. He had always been a dog who was wary of people, but with Jannie, he had taken to her right away, and it had been one of the ways Dash had known she was the one for him. Jet and Dash's bond was strong, and he never thought a woman could come and be accepted into it, but his faithful friend had welcomed her and loved her just as much as he had. They had instantly morphed into a settled and happy family.

Looking back now, the past month had flown by, and spending every day together had solidified their bond fast and true. He felt as if they had lived together for years, and each day brought with it new challenges and fun.

He enjoyed looking after and protecting his woman. And

she enjoyed looking after him. When he got home after a hard day up the mountain, on the search for the portal with the other wolves, dragons and bears, he could always count on a big juicy steak waiting for him and a large glass of red wine. Jannie thrived from giving him the best of her, and he thrived from giving her the best of him. Never before had he felt so complemented and settled.

To find his true other half had been the most incredible ride.

Jannie reached down and stroked Jet behind the ear, and then looked up and saw him watching her from the other side of the window. There was a moment that passed between them and in it, he saw his whole future. He saw the wolf cubs they would bring into the world. He saw the wedding they were planning, and he saw their children growing up in a safe town, where they didn't have to experience fear.

Jannie smiled and got to her feet, walking out to meet him on the veranda.

"Hey!" She smiled as he held out his arm and wrapped her under it. He pulled her close and breathed in the delicious scent of her hair.

There was literally nothing better than this. Just the two of them standing out there by the lake where they met, with all the magic and mystery of Bridge Hollow around them.

He kissed the top of her head and smiled.

Jet trotted out to them and sat next to Dash's feet. They all looked out across the lake to the old cabin and at the new people who had come to lease it. They had helped them on their first week in town and shown them some of the good places to go... Jannie had made Dash swear he wouldn't direct them to the dive bar on the highway, and he had agreed with a hearty laugh. That was already one of their secret jokes that they vowed never to reveal when anyone asked them about their first date. It was something just for them and their memories.

Dash knew there was a long way for them to go, and he still feared for Jannie's safety, but now that he had claimed her, he also knew that, if she were ever in danger, he would know within a split second. Their bond was strong and unbreakable, and he could find her anywhere on Earth in the skip of a heartbeat. She was his and he was hers, and together they were a force so powerful they felt ready for whatever life had to throw their way.

Jannie looked up at him and smiled, and Dash's eyes glinted green.

Their little part of the world was absolute perfection. And neither of them would ever want to be anywhere else.

Bridge Hollow was home, and now, it always would be.

* * *

WE HOPE YOU LOVED ALPHA PROTECTOR WOLF! IF SO THEN you will definitely want to check out the next book in the series!

Click her to get Fated Mate Daddy Bear on Amazon...

OR IF YOU STILL AREN'T CONVINCED, OF COURSE WE HAVE A brief preview...

THE SEARCH PARTY HAD BEEN COMBING THE MOUNTAINSIDE since the early hours of the morning. They had witnessed the dawn fog rolling in, the chill in the air, and the sun finally rising in the distance. They had watched from their various vantage points, wondering if this would keep happening in their part of the world or they would soon be doomed to eternal darkness.

Anson raised his hands and hooked them behind his head as he looked out across the mountain at the magnificent scene ahead of him. He had spent his morning climbing with the rest of his pack, surveying the forests and woodlands, checking and prepping for the next wave of terror to head their way.

They all hoped it wouldn't happen, but these shifter boys knew their stuff. And they could all feel it.

With the cold air of October, Bridge Hollow was also gripped with another fresh set of threats. Somewhere, a storm was brewing for them, and they had to be ready. For what could easily pose as a sleepy mountain town to the outside world, they sure had a lot going on when it came to drama. They may have had a reputation for their strange phenomena, but the tourists came in droves to feel excitement, not necessarily to find something paranormal. Since the beginning of the year, however, Bridge Hollow had been coming up trumps in that department.

The whole town was morphing before the resident's very eyes.

Each day brought uncertainty and more fear. And now, it was up to the shifter packs of the town to make sure everyone stayed safe.

His fellow pack members were a few hundred meters away sniffing the air, and Anson watched them. Even in their human form the way they picked up scents was heightened, and they had used it to their advantage since they had begun their search.

"What do you think?" Ryder asked him as they looked out at the snow-capped mountain. "Are we going up, or back down?"

Anson looked over his shoulder to the rest of the pack. If he was honest, he didn't think there was any need to go higher.

"The dragons would have found it by now," he said as he looked to the clouds and the top of the mountain range. "They spend the majority of their time hidden away up there… Surely, they would have noticed something."

Ryder nodded.

The two men turned and began to walk quickly down the slope toward the rest of the pack and then on to town. After all their searching and switching shifts with the wolves, still no one had found what they were looking for. And now, they were all beginning to get weary. For weeks, they had been searching for answers, for a place they were yet to understand but knew they had to find.

And it had eluded them every time.

Bridge Hollow had turned on all of them. There was danger waiting in the wings, ready to seize them. But the bears and wolves were prepared. They had to be. If they didn't stay two steps ahead, then they were all doomed.

The pack delved into the thick woodland as they made their way down to town, and they all stopped and pricked their ears as they came to the site of where the last tragedy had happened. Anson felt the chill roll through him, right down to the very center of his bones. It still felt like only a moment had passed since the vampire had waited for them. He had been a threat so wild and frightening, none of them had seen him coming. True evil had found its way to them, and even though they had defeated it this time, they knew more was to come.

"Come on," Anson said as he looked away from the clearing in the trees where the showdown had taken place. Even though it had been weeks before, he could still see the charred scar on the ground where they had killed the vampire. And he didn't want to remember it all over again.

He carried on walking with his shoulders held back and his head high. He was a strong bear, a protector of this town, and now that he had a taste of what was to come, he was certain he wasn't going to let his life be shattered.

He had too much to lose.

As they reached the beginnings of the log cabins and the last mountain roads that gave way to the more major route into town, Anson felt a rush of warmth and relief.

This was home.

It always would be.

He smiled as he ran a big, rough hand through his shaggy, brown hair and he thought of all he had to love here. His wonderful little world at home that he would die for.

He turned back and raised his hand to wave at Ryder and the other bears and then sloped off down his street to his cabin.

It was time for him to call it a day, to leave his brotherhood behind, but return to his other family. The one that had his whole heart.

His boots scuffed the ground as he walked past his red truck, and he laughed at the crumpled pink bike with its training wheels that had been abandoned in a pile by the front door. Already from inside he could hear the laughing and girly voice of his daughter and it made his eyes water with happiness.

He reached for the handle and opened it, and as he

stepped inside his home, he saw her turn and her eyes glint as she ran to him.

"Daddy!" she called as she scrambled down the hallway and jumped into his arms. He held her tight as she wrapped her arms around his neck and nuzzled her face in the stubbly beard on his chin.

"Hey, little darling," he said warmly as he looked into the kitchen to see his old aunt smiling back at him…

CONTINUE FATED MATE DADDY BEAR HERE ON AMAZON…